D1621280

S

CRAM

MIDWIVES ON-CALL

Welcome to Melbourne Victoria Hospital—
and to the exceptional midwives
who make up the Melbourne Maternity Unit!

These midwives in a million work miracles
on a daily basis, delivering tiny bundles of joy
into the arms of their brand-new mums!

Amidst the drama and emotion of babies
arriving at all hours of the day and night, when
the shifts are over, somehow there's still time
for some sizzling out-of-hours romance...

Whilst these caring professionals might come
face-to-face with a whole lot of love in their
line of work, now it's their turn to find
a happy-ever-after of their own!

Midwives On-Call

Midwives, mothers and babies—
lives changing for ever...!

Dear Reader,

I'm so excited to have written one of the *Midwives On-Call* continuity stories set in Melbourne.

When Kiwis visit Australia we call it hopping across the ditch. In this case my story has hopped over there. It's fun to write a story set in a very different location from my usual haunts.

Flynn and Ally are made for each other— it just takes them time to work that out. But who could go wrong with love on the beautiful Phillip Island, which sits just below Melbourne and the Victoria coastline? Throw in the cutest little boy and a big friendly dog and life's a beach.

I hope you enjoy reading Flynn and Ally's story, and seeing how it ties in with the other stories in this series.

Drop by my website, suemackay.co.nz, or send me an email at sue.mackay56@yahoo.com

Cheers!

Sue MacKay

MIDWIFE...
TO MUM!

BY
SUE MacKAY

First published in Great Britain 2015
by Mills & Boon, an imprint of Harlequin (UK) Limited,
Large Print edition 2015
Eton House, 18-24 Paradise Road,
Richmond, Surrey, TW9 1SR

© 2015 Harlequin Books S.A.

Special thanks and acknowledgement are given to Sue MacKay for her contribution to the Midwives On-Call series.

ISBN: 978-0-263-25516-4

Printed and bound in Great Britain
by CPI Antony Rowe, Chippenham, Wiltshire

With a background of working in medical laboratories, and a love of the romance genre, it is no surprise that **Sue MacKay** writes Mills & Boon Medical Romance stories. An avid reader all her life, she wrote her first story at age eight—about a prince, of course. She lives with her own hero in the beautiful Marlborough Sounds, at the top of New Zealand's South Island, where she indulges her passions for the outdoors, the sea and cycling.

Books by Sue MacKay

Mills & Boon Medical Romance

Doctors to Daddies

A Father for Her Baby
The Midwife's Son

The Family She Needs
A Family This Christmas
From Duty to Daddy
The Gift of a Child
You, Me and a Family
Christmas with Dr Delicious
Every Boy's Dream Dad
The Dangers of Dating Your Boss
Surgeon in a Wedding Dress

Visit the Author Profile page
at millsandboon.co.uk for more titles.

Praise for Sue MacKay

'A deeply emotional, heart-rending story that will make you smile and make you cry. I truly recommend it and don't miss the second book: the story about Max.'
—*HarlequinJunkie* on
The Gift of a Child

'What a great book. I loved it. I did not want it to end. This is one book not to miss.'
—*GoodReads* on
The Gift of a Child

MIDWIVES ON-CALL

Midwives, mothers and babies—
lives changing for ever…!

Enter the magical world of the Melbourne Maternity Unit and the exceptional midwives there, delivering tiny bundles of joy on a daily basis. Now it's time to find a happy-ever-after of their own…

Just One Night? by Carol Marinelli
Gorgeous Greek doctor Alessi Manos is determined
to charm the beautiful yet frosty Isla Delamere…
but can he melt this ice queen's heart?

Meant-To-Be Family by Marion Lennox
When Dr Oliver Evans's estranged wife, Emily, crashes back
into his life, old passions are reignited. But brilliant Dr Evans
is in for a surprise… Emily has two foster children!

Always the Midwife by Alison Roberts
Midwife Sophia Toulson and hard-working paramedic
Aiden Harrison share an explosive attraction…but will they
overcome their tragic pasts and take a chance on love?

Midwife's Baby Bump by Susanne Hampton
Hotshot surgeon Tristan Hamilton's passionate night
with pretty student midwife Flick has unexpected consequences!

Midwife…to Mum! by Sue MacKay
Free-spirited locum midwife Ally Parker
meets top GP and gorgeous single dad Flynn Reynolds.
Is she finally ready to settle down with a family of her own?

His Best Friend's Baby by Susan Carlisle
When beautiful redhead Phoebe Taylor turns up on ex-army medic
Ryan Matthews's doorstep there's only one thing keeping them apart:
she's his best friend's widow…and eight months pregnant!

Unlocking Her Surgeon's Heart by Fiona Lowe
Brooding city surgeon Noah Jackson
meets compassionate Outback midwife Lilia Cartwright.
Could Lilia be the key to Noah's locked-away heart?

Her Playboy's Secret by Tina Beckett
Renowned English obstetrician Darcie Green
might think playboy Lucas Elliot is nothing but trouble—
but is there more to this gorgeous doc than meets the eye?

Experience heartwarming emotion and pulse-racing drama in
Midwives On-Call
this sensational eight-book continuity
from Mills & Boon Medical Romance

These books are also available in eBook format
from millsandboon.co.uk

CHAPTER ONE

ALYSSA PARKER DROPPED her bags in the middle of the lounge and stared around what would be her next temporary living quarters. She could pretty much see it all from where she stood. Dusting and vacuuming weren't going to take up her spare time, like it had at the last place. She'd have to find something else to keep her busy after work. Take up knitting? Or hire a dog to walk every day?

Her phone rang. Tugging it from her jacket pocket, she read the name on the screen and punched the 'talk' button. 'Hey, boss, I've arrived on Phillip Island.' The bus trip down from Melbourne city had been interminable as she'd kept dozing off. It had taken the ferry crossing and lots of fresh air to clear her head.

'How's the head?' Lucas Elliot, her senior mid-wife, asked.

'It's good now. Who have you been talking to?'

She and some of the crew from the Melbourne Midwifery Unit had gone out for drinks, which had extended to a meal and more drinks.

'My lips are sealed,' Lucas quipped. 'So, Phillip Island—another place for you to tick off on the map.'

'Yep.' Her life was all about new destinations and experiences. Certainly not the regular nine to five in the same place, year in, year out, that most people preferred.

'How's the flat?'

'About the size of a dog kennel.' Stepping sideways, Ally peered into what looked like an overgrown cupboard. 'It's an exaggeration to call this a kitchen. But, hey, that's part of the adventure.' Like she needed a kitchen when she favoured takeout food anyway.

'Ally, I forgot to tell you where the key to the flat would be, but it seems you've taken up breaking and entering on the side.'

She was Ally to everyone except the taxman and her lawyer. And the social welfare system. 'It was under the pot plant on the top step.' The first place she'd looked.

'Why do people do that? It's so obvious.' Lucas sounded genuinely perplexed.

Still looking around, she muttered, 'I doubt there's much worth stealing in here.' Kat, the midwife she was replacing temporarily, certainly didn't spend her pay packet on home comforts.

'Are you happy with the arrangements? I know you enjoy everywhere we send you, but this should be the best yet as far as location goes. All those beaches to play on.'

'It's winter, or haven't you noticed?' Ally shook her head. 'But so far the island's looking beautiful.'

His chuckle was infectious. 'I'll leave you to unpack and find your way around. You're expected at the medical centre at eight thirty tomorrow. Dr Reynolds wants to run through a few details with you before you get started with the Monday morning antenatal list.'

'Same as any locum job I do, then?' She couldn't help the jibe. She'd been doing this relief work for two years now. It suited her roving lifestyle perfectly and was the only reason she remained with the Melbourne Midwifery Unit. They'd offered her fixed positions time and again. She'd turned them all down. Fixed meant working continuously at the midwifery unit, which in turn meant getting too close to those people she'd work with every day.

The days when she set herself up to get dumped by anyone—friends, colleagues or lovers—were long over. Had been from the monumental day she'd turned sixteen and taken control of her life. She'd walked out of the social welfare building for the very last time. It hadn't mattered that she'd had little money or knowledge on how to survive. She'd known a sense of wonder at being in charge of herself. Since then no one had screwed up her expectations because she'd been in charge of her own destiny. Because she hadn't allowed herself to hope for family or love again.

'I'm being pedantic.' Lucas was still on the other end of the line. 'I wanted to make sure everything's okay.'

Why wouldn't it be? She didn't need him fussing about her. She didn't like it. It spoke of care and concern. But Lucas did care about the people he worked with, which, despite trying not to let it, had always warmed her and given her a sense of belonging to the unit. Since she didn't do belonging, it showed how good Lucas was with his staff.

She told him, 'I'll take a walk to get my bearings and suss out where the medical centre is as soon as I've unpacked.' Tomorrow she'd collect the car provided for the job.

'Even your map-reading skills might just about manage that.' He laughed at his own joke. 'I'll leave you to get settled. Catch you in four weeks, unless there's a problem.'

Stuffing the phone back in her pocket, she headed into the bedroom and dumped a bag on the bed. At least it was a double. Not that she had any man to share the other half with. Not yet. *Who knows? There might be a hot guy at the surf beach who'd like a short fling, no strings.* Her mouth watered at the thought of all those muscles surfers must have. Winter wouldn't stop those dudes getting on their boards. There were such things as wetsuits.

After dropping her second, smaller bag full of books and DVDs out of the way in the corner of the lounge, she slapped her hands on her hips and stared around. Four o'clock in the afternoon and nothing to do. Once she started on the job she'd be fine, but these first hours when she arrived in a new place and moved into someone else's home always made her feel antsy. It wasn't her space, didn't hold her favourite possessions.

Except… Unzipping the bag, she placed two small silver statues on the only shelf. 'Hey, guys, welcome to Cowes.' Her finger traced the outlines of her pets. If she ever got to own a pet it would be a springer spaniel like these. Make that two spaniels. One on its own would be lonely.

She hadn't forgiven the Bartlett family who'd given her these on the day they'd broken her heart, along with their promise they'd love her for ever. She'd wrapped the statues in an empty chocolate box and tied it with a yellow ribbon, before burying them in the Bartletts' garden. The gift had been a consolation prize for abandoning her, but one dark day when she'd felt unable to carry on, she'd remembered the dogs *she'd* abandoned and had sneaked back to retrieve them. They'd gone everywhere with her ever since, a talisman to her stronger self.

Having the statues in place didn't make the flat hers, though. Again Ally stared around. She could do a lap of the cupboards and shelves, learning where everything was kept. By then it'd be five past four and she'd still not know what to do with herself.

This moment was the only time she ever allowed that her life wasn't normal. *Define normal.* Doing what other people did.

Standing in the middle of a home she'd never been in before, didn't know the owner of, always brought up the question of what would it be like to settle down for ever in her own place.

As if she'd ever do that.

What if it was with a man who loved me regardless?

The answer never changed. That person didn't exist.

She followed her established routine for first days in new towns. First, off came her new and amazing knee-high black boots, then she pulled on her top-of-the-line walking shoes.

Sliding on her sunglasses, she snatched up the house key and stuffed it and her wallet into her pocket and headed out. There had to be a decent coffee shop somewhere. Might as well check out the options for takeout dinners, too. Then she'd head to the nearest beach to do some exploring.

The coffee turned out to be better than good. Ally drained the paper mug of every last drop and tossed it into the next rubbish bin she came across. The beach stretched ahead as she kicked up sand and watched the sea relentlessly rolling in. Kids chased balls and each other, couples strolled hand in hand, one grown-up idiot raced into the freezing water and straight back out, shouting his head off in shock.

Ally pulled out her phone and called the midwifery centre back in the city, sighing happily when Darcie answered. 'Hey, how's the head?'

'Nothing wrong with mine, but, then, I was on orange juice all night.'

'You shouldn't be so quick to put your hand up for call.'

Darcie grumped, 'Says the woman who works more hours than the rest of us.' Then she cheered Ally up with, 'You can move into my spare room when you get back to town. As of this morning it's empty, my flatmate having found her own place.'

'Great, that's cool.' Darcie was fast becoming a good friend, which did bother her when she thought about it. But right this moment it felt good to have a friend onside when she was feeling more unsettled than usual at the start of a new assignment. Today she sensed she might be missing out on the bigger picture. This was the loneliness she'd learned to cope with whenever she'd been shuffled off to yet another foster home full of well-meaning people who'd always eventually packed her bags and sent her away.

'You still there?' Darcie asked.

'Did you get called in today?'

'I've just finished an urgent caesarean, and I'm about to get something to eat.'

'I'll leave you to it, then. Thanks for the bed. I'll definitely take you up on that.' After saying goodbye, she shoved her hands deep into her jacket pockets and began striding to the farthest end of the beach, feeling better already. Being alone wasn't so bad when there were people at the end of a phone. At least this way she got to choose which side of the bed she slept on, what she had for dinner, and when to move on to the next stop.

A ball came straight for her and she lined it up, kicked it back hard, aiming for the boys running after it. One of them swung a foot at it and missed, much to his mates' mirth at a girl kicking it better.

'Girls can do anything better.' She grinned and continued walking a few metres above the water's edge, feeling happier by the minute. How could she remain gloomy out here? The beach was beautiful, the air fresh, and she had a new job in the morning. What else could she possibly need?

The sun began dropping fast and Ally stopped to watch the amazing reds and yellows spreading, blending the sky and water into one molten colour block, like a young child's painting. Her throat ached with the beauty of it.

Thud. Something solid slammed into her. For a moment, as she teetered on her feet, she thought she'd keep her balance. But another shove and she toppled into an ungainly heap on the sand with the heavy weight on top of her. A moving, panting, licking heavy weight. A dog of no mean proportions with gross doggy breath sprawled across her.

'Hey, get off me.' She squirmed between paws and tried to push upright onto her backside.

One paw shoved her back down, and the dark,

furry head blocked out all vision of the sunset. The rear end of the animal was wriggling back and forth as its tail whipped through the air.

'Sheba, come here.' A male voice came from somewhere above them. 'Get off now.'

Sheba—if that was the name of her assailant—gave Ally's chin a final lick and leapt sideways, avoiding an outstretched hand that must've been aiming for her collar.

'Phew.'

Her relief was premature. The dog lay down beside her as close as possible, and farthest away from the man trying to catch her. One paw banged down on her stomach, forcing all the air out of her lungs.

Somewhere behind her a young child started laughing. 'Sheba, you're funny.'

The sweet childish sound of pure enjoyment had Ally carefully pushing the paw aside and sitting up to look round for the source. A cute little boy was leaping up and down, giggling fit to bust.

'Sheba. Sit now.' The man wasn't nearly as thrilled about his dog's behaviour.

Ally stared up at the guy looming above her.

'It's all right. I'm fine, really.' She even smiled to prove her point.

'I'm very sorry Sheba bowled you over. She doesn't understand her own strength.' As he glanced across at the child his annoyance was quickly replaced by something soft she couldn't read. 'Adam, don't encourage her.'

'But it's funny, Dad.' The boy folded in half, still giggling.

Ally clambered to her feet, dusting sand off her jeans, and grinned. 'What is it about kids and giggling? They don't seem to know how to stop.' Just watching the boy made her happy—especially now that the dog had loped across to bunt him in the bottom, which only made the giggles louder. Laughter threatened to bubble up from deep inside her stomach.

The guy was shaking his head, looking bemused. 'Beats me how he keeps going so long.'

Ally winced. Slapping the sand off her left hip just made it sore. Sheba must've bruised her.

'Are you all right?' the man asked, worry darkening his expression. 'Look, I apologise again. I hope you haven't been hurt.'

'Look,' she used his word back at him. 'I'm

fine. Seriously. Sheba was being playful and if I hadn't been staring at the sunset I'd have seen her coming.' She stuck her hand out. 'I'm Ally. That's Sheba, and your boy's called Adam. You are?'

'Flynn. We've been visiting friends all day and needed some fresh air before settling down for the night.' He looked at her properly, finally letting go the need to watch his boy and dog. 'What about you?'

'Much the same. The beach is hard to resist when the weather's so balmy.' He didn't need to know she'd only just arrived. Running her hands over the sleeves of her jacket, she smoothed off the remaining sand, trying to refrain from staring at him. But it was impossible to look away.

Despite the sadness in his eyes, or because of it, she was taking more notice of him than a casual meeting on the beach usually entailed. The stubble darkening his chin was downright sexy, while that tousled hair brought heat to her cold cheeks. If she played her cards right, could this be the man she had her next fling with?

She glanced downward, taking in his athletic build, his fitted jeans that defined many of his muscles. The sun glinted off something on the guy's hand and she had her answer. A band of gold. Said it all, really.

'Can I call you Ally?' Adam bounced up in front of her.

Blink, blink. Refocus on the younger version now that the older one was out of bounds. 'Of course you can.' As if they were going to see each other again. Though they might, she realised, if Flynn brought his son to the beach often. She'd be walking along here most days that she wasn't caught up with delivering babies and talking to pregnant mums.

Hopefully, if they ran into each other again, Flynn would have his wife with him. A wife would certainly dampen the flare of attraction that had snagged her, and which should've evaporated the moment she'd seen that ring. Flings were the way to go, but never, ever with a man already involved with someone else. She didn't do hurting for the sake of it, or for any reason at all, come to think of it.

Guess she'd have to keep looking for someone to warm the other half of that bed. *Whoa,*

Ally, you haven't been here more than an hour. What's the hurry?

The thing was, if she was playing bed games there wouldn't be long, empty nights that had her dreaming of the impossible. She could shove the overpowering sense of unworthiness aside as she and a man made each other happy for a short while, and then bury her face in the pillow while he left. Every parting, even as casual as her relationships were, was touched with a longing for the life she craved, had never known, and was too afraid to try for.

Flynn Reynolds dragged his gaze away from the most attractive woman he'd met in a long while and focused on his son. Except Adam stood directly in front of her, talking nonstop, and Flynn's gaze easily moved across the tiny gap to a stunning pair of legs clad in skin-tight jeans. His breathing hitched in his throat. Oh, wow. Gorgeous.

The woman—*Ally, she has a name*—laughed at something Adam said, a deep, pure laugh that spoke of enjoyment with no hidden agenda. Very refreshing, considering most women he met these days seemed intent on luring him into their clutches with false concern about him and Adam. He hated it that many women believed the way to attract him was by being overfriendly to his son. What they didn't get was that Adam saw through them almost as quickly as he did.

What they also didn't get was that Flynn wasn't interested. Not at all. So why was his gaze cruising over the length of this curvy woman with a smile that had him smiling back immediately, even when it wasn't directed at him? Especially since he apparently didn't do smiling very much these days.

He looked directly at his son. 'Time we made tracks for home. The sun's nearly gone and it will be cold soon.' Any excuse to cut this short and put some space between him and Ally before his brain started thinking along the lines of wanting to get to know her better. He wasn't ready for another woman in his life. Certainly wouldn't have time for years to come, either.

'Do we have to?'

'Yes, I'm afraid so.'

What I'm really afraid of is staying to talk to Ally too long and ending up inviting her home

*to share dinner with us. If she's free and avail-
able.* As if a woman as attractive as her would
be seriously single. The absence of rings on her
fingers didn't mean a thing.

He looked around and groaned. 'Sheba,' he
yelled. 'Come here.'

Too late. The mutt was belly deep in the sea,
leaping and splashing without any concern for
how cold the water had to be.

Adam ran down to the water's edge and stood
with his hands on his skinny hips. 'Sheba, Dad
says we're going home. You want your dinner?'

Beside Flynn, Ally chuckled. 'Good luck with
that.'

Glancing at her, he drew a deep breath. Her
cheeks had flushed deep pink when the mutt
had dumped her on the sand, and the colour
still remained, becoming rosier every time she
laughed. Which was often.

He noticed her rubbing her hip. 'You did hurt
yourself.'

She jammed her hand in her pocket. 'Just a
hard landing, nothing to worry about.'

'You're sure?' He'd hate it if Sheba had caused
some damage.

'Absolutely.'

Adam and Sheba romped up to him. Then the dog did what wet dogs did—shook herself hard, sending salty spray over everyone. Now Ally would complain and walk away. But no. Her laughter filled the air and warmed the permanent chill in his soul. It would be unbelievably easy to get entangled with someone like her. Make that with this woman in particular.

He sighed his disappointment. There was no room in his life for a woman, no matter how beautiful. Not even for a short time. Adam and work demanded all his attention. Besides, how did a guy go about dating? He hadn't been in that market for so long he wouldn't know where to start. Was there a dating book for dummies? *I don't need one. It's not happening.* He gave himself a mental slap. All these questions and doubts because of a woman he'd met five minutes ago. He was in need of a break. That was his real problem. Solo parenting and work gobbled up all his time and energy.

'Let's go.' He grabbed Sheba's collar and turned in the direction of their street. 'Nice meeting you.' He nodded abruptly at the woman who'd been the first one to catch his interest since Anna had died two years ago. It had to be a fleeting interest; one that would've disappeared by the time he reached home and became immersed in preparing dinner, folding washing and getting ready for work tomorrow. Damn it all. It could've been fun getting to know her.

'Bye, Ally,' Adam called, as they started walking up the beach.

She stood watching them, both hands in her jacket pockets. 'See you around.' Was that a hint of wistfulness in her voice?

'Okay,' Adam answered, apparently reluctant to leave her. 'Tomorrow?'

'Adam,' Flynn growled. 'Come on.' He aimed for the road, deliberately stamping down on the urge to invite the woman home to share dinner. He did not need anyone else's problems. He did not need anyone else, full stop.

Anyway, she probably wouldn't like baked beans on toast.

Baked beans. He only had to close his eyes to hear Anna saying how unhealthy they were.

They'd eaten lots of vegetables for lunch so he could relax the rules tonight. Beans once in a while wouldn't hurt Adam, and would save *him* some time. Who knew? He might get to watch the late news. Life was really looking up.

CHAPTER TWO

PLASTERING ON HER best smiley face the next morning, Ally stepped inside the medical centre, unzipping her jacket as she crossed to the reception desk. 'Hi, I'm Alyssa Parker.' Lucas always wrote her full name on her credentials when sending them to medical centres. It was a technicality he adhered to, and she hated it. 'Ally for short. I'm covering for Kat while she's away.'

A man straightened from the file he was reading and she gasped as the piercing blue eyes that had followed her into sleep last night now scanned her. Her smile widened. 'Flynn.' The buzz she'd felt standing by this man yesterday returned in full force, fizzing through her veins, heating her in places she definitely didn't need warmed by a married man. He was still as sexy, despite the stubble having been shaved off. *Stop it*. But she'd have to be six feet under not to react to him.

'Ally. Or do you prefer Alyssa?'

'Definitely Ally. Never Alyssa. So you're Dr Reynolds?' They hadn't swapped surnames the previous day. Hardly been any point when the chances of meeting again had seemed remote. Neither had she learned his first name when she was told about this job. She became aware of the receptionist glancing from her to Flynn, eyebrows high and a calculating look in her eyes.

Fortunately Flynn must've seen her, too. 'Megan's our office lady and general everything girl. She'll help you find files and stock lists and anything else you want.'

'You two know each other?' Megan asked her burning question.

Ally left that to Flynn to deal with and took a quick look around the office, but listened in as Flynn told the receptionist, 'We met briefly yesterday. Can you tell the others as they arrive that we're in the tearoom and can they come along to meet Ally?' Then he joined her on the other side of the counter. 'I'll show you around. You've got a busy clinic this morning. Three near full-term mums and four who are in their second trimester.'

'Three close to full term? Was there a party on the island eight months back that everyone went to?' She grinned.

'You'd be surprised how many pregnant ladies we see. Phillip Island's population isn't as small as people think. One of the women, Marie Canton, is Adam's daytime caregiver when he's not at preschool.'

So Adam's mum worked, too. Ally wondered what she did. A doctor, like her husband? 'Will Marie be bringing Adam with her?'

'I'm not sure.'

'What time's my first appointment?' she asked, suddenly needing to stay on track and be professional.

But Flynn smiled, and instantly ramped up that heat circulating her body, defying her professionalism. 'Nine. Was it explained to you that Kat also does high school visits to talk to the teenagers about contraception?' Flynn stood back and indicated with a wave of his hand for her to precede him into a kitchen-cum-meeting-room. 'You've got one on Thursday afternoon.'

'I didn't know, but not a problem.' What was that aftershave? She sniffed a second time, savouring the tangy scent that reminded her of the outdoors and sun and…? And hot male. She tripped over her size sevens and grabbed the back of a chair to regain her balance. 'I'm still breaking these boots in,' she explained quickly, hoping Flynn wouldn't notice the sudden glow in her cheeks. He mustn't think she was clumsy but, worse, he mustn't guess what had nearly sent her crashing face first onto the floor.

But when she glanced at him she relaxed. His gaze was firmly fixed on the boots she'd blamed. Her awesome new boots that had cost nearly a week's pay. His eyes widened, then cruised slowly, too slowly, up her thighs to her hips, up, up, up, until he finally locked gazes with her. So much for relaxing. Now she felt as though she was in a sauna and there was no way out. The heat just kept getting steamier. Her tongue felt too big for her mouth. Her eyes must look like bug's eyes; they certainly felt as though they were out on stalks.

Flynn was one sexy unit. The air between them sparked like electricity. His hair was as tousled as it had been yesterday and just as tempting. Her fingers curled into her palms, her false nails digging deep into her skin as she fought not to reach out and finger-comb those thick waves.

'You must be the midwife.' A woman in her midforties suddenly appeared before her. 'Faye Bellamy, part-time GP for my sins.'

Ally took a step back to put space between her and Flynn, and reached for Faye's proffered hand. 'That's me. Ally Parker. Pleased to meet you.'

'Pleasure's all ours. Darned nuisance Kat wanting time off, but I've read your résumé and it seems you'll be a perfect fit for her job.' Bang, mugs hit the benchtop. 'Coffee, everyone?'

Kat wasn't meant to take holidays? Or just this one? 'Yes, thanks. Where's Kat gone?'

Flynn was quick to answer. 'To Holland for her great-grandmother's ninetieth birthday. She's been saving her leave for this trip.' He flicked a glance at Faye's back, then looked at Ally. 'She could've taken two months and still not used up what she's owed,' he added.

'Europe's a long way to go for any less time.' Not that it had anything to do with her, except she would have been signed on here for longer and that meant more weeks—okay, hours—in

Flynn's company. Already that looked like being a problem. His marital status wasn't having any effect on curtailing the reaction her body had to him.

She took the mug being handed to her and was surprised to see her hand shaking. She searched her head for something ordinary to focus on, and came back to Kat. 'Bet the trip's another reason why there isn't much furniture or clutter in the flat.' A girl after her own heart, though for a different reason.

'Morning, everyone.' A man strolled in. 'Coffee smells good.' Then he saw Ally. 'Hi, I'm Jerome, GP extraordinaire, working with this motley lot.'

Amidst laughter and banter Ally sat back and listened as the nurses joined them and began discussing patients and the two emergencies that had happened over the weekend. She felt right at home. This was the same Monday-morning scenario she'd sat through in most of the clinics she'd worked at ever since qualifying. Same cases, different names. Same egos, different names. Soon her gaze wandered to the man sitting opposite her, and she felt that hitch in her breathing again.

Flynn was watching her from under hooded eyes, his chin low, his arms folded across his chest as he leaned as far back in his chair as possible without spilling over backwards.

Ally's breathing became shallow and fast, like it did after a particularly hard run. The man had no right to make her feel like this. Who did he think he was? The sooner this meeting was finished the better. She could go and play with patients and hide from him until all her body parts returned to their normal functions. At the rate she was going, that'd be some time around midnight.

The sound of scraping chairs on the floor dragged her attention back to the other people in the room and gave her the escape she desperately needed.

But fifteen minutes after the meeting ended, Flynn was entering her room with a frightened young girl in tow. 'Ally, I'd like you to meet Chrissie Gordon.' He ushered the girl, dressed in school uniform, to a chair.

'Hi, Chrissie. Love your nail colour. It's like

hot pink and fiery red all mixed up.' It would have lit up a dark room.

'It's called Monster Red.' Chrissie shrugged at her, as if to say, Who gives a rat's tail? Something serious was definitely on this young lady's mind.

Given that Flynn had brought Chrissie to see *her*, they must be about to talk about protection during sex or STDs. Or pregnancy. The girl looked stumped, as if her worst possible nightmare had just become real. Ally wanted to scoop her up into her arms and ward off whatever was about to be revealed. Instead, she looked at Flynn and raised an eyebrow.

'Chrissie's done several dip-stick tests for pregnancy and they all showed positive.' Flynn's face held nothing but sympathy for his patient's predicament. 'I'd like you to take a blood sample for an HCG test to confirm that, and then we'll also know how far along she is if the result's positive.'

It wasn't going to be negative with all those stick tests showing otherwise. 'No problem.'

Ally took the lab form he handed her and glancing down saw requests for WR and VDRL to check for STDs, antibodies and a blood group.

She noted the girl's date of birth. Chrissie was fifteen. Too young to be dealing with this. Ally's heart went out to the frightened child as she thought back to when she'd been that age. She'd barely been coping with her own life, let alone be able to manage looking after a baby. Face it, she doubted her ability to do that *now*. Locking eyes with Flynn, she said, 'Leave it to me.'

His nod was sharp. 'Right, Chrissie, I'll call you on your cell when the lab results come back.'

'Thanks, Dr Reynolds,' Chrissie whispered, as her fingers picked at the edge of her jersey, beginning to unravel a thread. 'You won't tell Mum, will you?'

'Of course not. You know even if I wanted to—which I don't—I'm not allowed to disclose your confidential information. It's up to you to decide when to talk to your mother, but let's wait until we get these tests done and you can come and see me again first, if that'll make it easier for you.' Flynn drew a breath and added, 'You won't be able to hide the pregnancy for ever.'

'I know. But not yet, okay?' The girl's head bowed over her almost flat chest. 'I'm afraid. It hurts to have a baby, doesn't it?'

Ally placed a hand over Chrissie's and squeezed gently. 'You're getting way ahead of yourself. Let's do those tests and find out how far along you are. After I've taken your blood I'll explain a few things about early-stage pregnancy if you like.'

'Yes, please. I think.' Fat tears oozed out of Chrissie's eyes and slid down her cheeks to drip onto her jersey. 'Mum's going to kill me.'

'No, she won't,' Flynn said. About to leave the room, he turned back to hunker down in front of Chrissie and said emphatically, 'Angela will be very supportive of you. You're her daughter. That's what mothers do.'

Yeah, right, you don't know a thing, buster, if that's what you believe. Did you grow up in la-la land? Ally clamped her lips shut for fear of spilling the truth. *Some mothers couldn't care two drops of nothing about their daughters. Some dump their babies on strangers' doorsteps.*

But when she glanced at Flynn, he shook his head and mouthed, 'It's true of Angela.'

Had he known what she'd been thinking? The tension that had been tightening her shoulders left off as she conceded silently that if he was right then Chrissie was luckier than some. A big positive in what must feel like a very negative morning for the girl. 'Good,' she acknowledged with a nod at Flynn. As for his mind-reading, did that mean he'd known exactly what she'd been thinking about him back there in the staffroom?

'Have you had a blood test before?' she asked Chrissie. She'd wasted enough time thinking about Dr Reynolds.

Flynn disappeared quietly, closing the door behind him.

'Yeah, three times. I hate them. I fainted every time.'

'You can lie on the bed, then. No way do I want to be picking you off the floor, now, do I?'

She was rewarded with a glimmer of a smile. 'I don't weigh too much. You'd manage.'

It was the first time anyone had suggested she looked tough and strong. 'I might manage, but me and weightlifting don't get along. How heavy are you anyway?'

'Forty-eight k. I'm lucky, I can eat and eat and I stay thin. My mum's jealous.' At the mention of her mum her face fell and her mouth puckered. 'I can't tell her. She'll be really angry. She had me when she was seventeen. All my life she's told me not to play around with boys. She wants me to go to university and be educated, unlike her. She missed out because she had me.'

Handing Chrissie a cup of cold water and a box of tissues, Ally sat down to talk. Her first booked appointment would have to wait. 'I won't deny your mother's going to be disappointed, even upset, but she'll come round because she loves you.' Flynn had better have got that right because she didn't believe in giving false hope. It just hurt more in the long run.

'You think? You don't even know her.'

'True. But I see a young woman who someone's been making sure had everything that's important in life. You look healthy, which means she's fed you well and kept you warm and clothed. Your uniform's in good condition, not an op-shop one. You're obviously up to speed with your education.' She daren't ask about her father. It didn't sound like he factored into Chrissie's current situation so maybe he didn't exist, or wasn't close enough for it to matter. 'I'm new here. Where do you live?'

'Round in San Remo. It's nice there. Grand-

dad was a fisherman and had a house so Mum
and I stayed with him. He's gone now and there's
just us. I miss him. He always had a hug and a
smile for me.'

'Then you've been very lucky. Not everyone gets those as they're growing up.' She sure
as heck hadn't. 'Let's get those blood samples
done.'

Chrissie paled but climbed onto the bed and
tugged one arm free of her jersey and shirt.
Lying down, she found a small scared smile.
'Be nice to me.'

Ally smiled. 'If I have to.' She could get to
really like this girl. Pointless when she'd be gone
in a month. Despite Chrissie's fear of what the
future had in store for her, she managed to be
friendly and not sulky, as most teens she'd met
in this situation had been.

Ally found the needle and tubes for the blood
in the top drawer of the cabinet beside the bed.
'Do you play any sport at school?' She swabbed
the skin where she would insert the needle.

'I'm in the school rep basketball team and play
soccer at the club. I get knocked about a bit in
basketball because I'm so light, but my elbows

are sharp.' The needle slid in and the tube began to fill. 'I'm fast on my feet. Learnt how to get out of the way when I was a kid and played rough games with the boys next door.'

Ally swapped the full tube for another one, this time for haematology tests. Flynn was checking Chrissie's haemoglobin in case she had anaemia. 'I see one of the beaches is popular for surfing. You ever given that a try?' All done.

'Everyone surfs around here. Sort of, anyway. Like belly-surfing and stuff.'

'You can sit up now.' Ally began labelling the tubes.

'What? Have you finished? I didn't feel a thing.'

'Of course you didn't.' She smiled at the girl, stopped when she saw the moment Chrissie's thoughts returned to why she was there, saw the tears building up again. 'You're doing fine.'

'I'm not going to play sport for a while, am I?'

'Maybe not competitively, but keeping fit is good for you and your baby.'

Chrissie blew hard into a handful of tissues. 'You haven't told me I'm stupid for getting caught out. Or asked who the father is, or anything like that.'

'That's irrelevant. I'm more concerned about making sure you do the right things to stay healthy and have an easy pregnancy. Have you got any questions for me?'

Chrissie swung her legs over the side of the bed and stared at the floor. 'Lots, but not yet. But can I come see you later? After school? You'll have the tests back by then, right?'

'The important one, anyway. But won't you want to see Dr Reynolds about that?' She was more than happy to tell Chrissie the result, but she had no idea how Flynn might feel if she did.

'He's going to phone me, but I might need to see someone and I don't want to talk to a man. It would be embarrassing. I'd prefer it's you.'

'That's okay.' Ally scribbled her cell number on a scrap of paper. 'Here, call me. Leave a message if I don't answer and I'll get back to you as soon as I'm free. Okay?'

'Thanks.' Sniff. 'I didn't sleep all night, hoping Dr Reynolds would tell me I'd got it wrong, that I wasn't having a baby. But I used up all my pocket money on testing kits and every one of them gave me the same answer so I was just being dumb.'

'Chrissie, listen to me. You are not dumb. Many women I've been midwife to have told me the same thing. Some of them because they couldn't believe their luck, others because, just like you, they were crossing their fingers and toes they'd got it wrong.' Ally drew a long breath. 'Chrissie, I have to ask, have you considered an abortion? Or adoption?'

The girl's head shot up, defiance spitting out of her eyes. 'No. Never.' Her hands went to her belly. 'This is my baby. No one else's. I might be young and dependent on Mum, but I am keeping it.'

In that moment Ally loved Chrissie. She reached over to hug her. 'Attagirl. You're awesome.' It would be the hardest thing Chrissie ever did, and right now she had no idea what she'd let herself in for, but that baby would love her for it.

'Have you ever had a baby?' Chrissie pulled back, flushing pink. 'Sorry, I guess I'm not supposed to want to know.'

'Of course it's all right to ask. The answer's no, I haven't.'

An image of a blue-eyed youngster bent over double and giggling like his life depended on it flicked up in her mind. *Go away, Adam. You've got a mother, and anyway I'd be a bad substitute.*

'So while I will tell you lots of things over the weeks I'm here, I only know them from working with other mums-to-be and not from any first-hand experience.' She would never have that accreditation on her CV. She would not raise a child on her own, and she wouldn't be trusting any man to hang around long enough to see a baby grow to adulthood with her.

Flynn appeared in the doorway so fast after Chrissie left that she wondered if he'd been lurking. She said, 'She's only fifteen and is terrified, and yet she's coping amazingly well, given the shock of it all.'

'You must've cheered her up a little at least. I got the glimmer of a smile when she came out of here.' He leaned one shoulder against the doorframe. 'I meant what I said about her mother. Angela is going to be gutted, but she'll stand by Chrissie all the way. From what I've been told, Angela's always been strong, and refused to marry Chrissie's dad just because people thought it was the done thing. Her father supported them all the way.'

Another baby with only one parent. But one decent parent was a hundred percent better than none. 'Aren't you jumping the gun? Chrissie didn't mention the father of her baby, but that could be because she's protecting him. They might want to stick together.'

'They might.' Flynn nodded, his eyes fixed on her. Again.

When he did that, her stomach tightened in a very needy way. Heat sizzled along her veins, warming every cell of her body. *Damn him. Why does he have to be married?*

'Right, I'd better see my first patient. First booked-in one, that is. I told Chrissie I'll talk to her later today. Is that all right with you?'

'Go for it. As long as she's talking with some-one, I'm happy. You did well with her.' There was something like admiration in his voice.

She didn't know whether to be pleased, or

annoyed that he might be surprised. 'Just doing my job.'

'Sure.'

The way he enunciated that one word had her wondering if he had issues with Kat and her work. But that didn't make sense after he'd been fighting the other woman's corner about using her holiday time. 'Being a filler-in person, I don't have the luxury of knowing the patients I see. Neither do I have a lot of time with them so I work hard to put them at ease with me as quickly as possible.'

'So why aren't you employed at a medical practice on a permanent basis? Wouldn't you prefer getting to know your mums, rather than moving on all the time?'

If he hadn't sounded so genuinely interested she'd have made a joke about being a wandering witch in a previous life and ignored the real question. But for some inexplicable reason she couldn't go past that sincerity. 'I get offers all the time from my bosses to base myself back at the midwifery unit, but I don't do settled in one spot very well. Yes, I miss out on seeing mothers going the distance. I'm only ever there for the beginning of some babies and the arrival of others, but I like it that way. Keeps me on my toes.'

'Fly in, do the job and fly out.' Was that a dash of hope in his eyes? Did he think she might be footloose and fancy-free enough to have a quick fling with him and then move on? Because she'd seen the same sizzle in his eyes that buzzed along her veins.

Then reality hit. Cold water being tipped over her wouldn't have chilled her as much. *Sorry, buster, but you're married and, worse, you're not even ashamed to show it.*

She spun around to stare at the screen in front of her. What was the name of her next patient?

'Ally, I've upset you.'

Of course he had. He only had to look at her to upset her—her hormones anyway. Flicking him a brief smile, she continued staring at the computer. 'Holly Sargent, thirty-five weeks. Anything I need to know about her that's not on here?'

When Flynn didn't answer, she had to lift her head and seek him out. That steady blue gaze was firmly fixed on her. It held far too many questions, and she didn't answer other people's enquiries about anything personal. 'Flynn? Holly Sargent?'

'Third pregnancy, the last two were straight-forward. She's had the usual colds and flu, a broken wrist and stitches in her brow from when she walked through a closed glass slider. Full-time mum.'

Ally looked at her patient list. 'Brenda Lewis?'

'First pregnancy, took six months to conceive, family history of hypertension but so far she's shown no signs of it, twenty-five years old, runs a local day care centre for under-fives.'

Her anger deflated and laughter bubbled up to spill between them as she stared at this man who had her all in a dither with very little effort. 'That's amazing. Do you know all your patients as thoroughly?'

'How long have you got?' He grinned. 'Makes for scintillating conversations.'

Deliberately rolling her eyes at him, she said, 'Remind me not to get stuck with you at the workplace Friday night drinkies.'

'Shucks, and I was about to ask you on a date,' he quipped, in a tone that said he meant no such thing.

So he was as confused as she was. That didn't stop a quick shiver running down her spine. She'd love to go out with this man. *But hello. If that isn't a wedding ring, then what is it? He's obviously a flagrant playboy.* 'Sorry, doing my hair that night.'

'Me, too,' he muttered, and left her to stare at his retreating back view.

A very delectable view at that. Those butt muscles moved smoothly under his trousers as he strode down the hall, those shoulders filled the top of his shirt to perfection. A sigh trickled over her bottom lip. He would've been the perfect candidate for her next affair. *Flynn might be the one you can't easily walk away from.*

'Get a grip, man,' Flynn growled under his breath. How? Ally was hot. Certain parts of his anatomy might've been in hibernation for the past couple of years, but they weren't dead. How did any sane, red-blooded male ignore Ally without going bonkers?

'Flynn.' Megan beckoned from the office. 'Can you explain to this caller why she should have a flu jab?'

'Can't Toby do that?' The practice nurse was more than capable of handling it.

'Busy with a patient and…' Megan put her hand over the phone's mouthpiece '…this one won't go away.'

'Put her through.' He spun around to head to his consulting room. *See? You're at work, not on the beach with nothing more important to think about than getting laid.* Forget all things Alyssa. *Alyssa.* Such a pretty name, but it had been blatantly obvious no one was allowed to use it when talking to their temporary midwife.

'Dr Reynolds.' Mrs Augusta's big voice boomed down the line, causing him to pull the phone away from his ear. 'I've been told I have to have a flu injection. I don't see why as I never get sick.'

Except for two hits with cancer that had nearly stolen her life. 'Mrs Augusta, it's your decision entirely but there are certain conditions whereby we recommend to a patient they have the vaccination. Your recent cancer puts you in the category for this. It's a preventative measure, that's all.'

'Why didn't Megan just tell me that?'

'Because she's our receptionist, not a qualified medical person. It's not her role to advise patients.'

'All right, can you put me back to her so I can book a time? Sorry to have been a nuisance.' Mrs Augusta suddenly sounded deflated, all the boom and bluster gone.

'Pat, is there something else that's bothering you?'

'No, I'm good as gold, Doctor. Don't you go worrying about me.'

'How about you make an appointment with me when you come for your jab?'

'I don't want to be a problem, Doctor.'

That exact attitude had almost cost her life. By the time the bowel cancer had been discovered it had nearly been too late and now she wore a bag permanently. 'I'll put you back to Megan and you make a time to see me.' When he got the receptionist on the line he told her, 'Book Mrs Augusta in with me at the first opening, and don't let her talk you out of it.'

A glance at his watch on his way out to the waiting room told him he was now behind the ball as far as keeping on time with appointments. 'Jane, come through.' As he led the woman down the hall, laughter came from the midwife's room. Sounded like Ally and Holly were getting along fine. A smile hovered on his mouth, gave him the warm fuzzies. Everyone got along with their temp midwife.

Jane limped into his room on her walking cane and sat down heavily. 'I'm up the duff again, Flynn.'

Not even ten o'clock and his second pregnant patient of the morning. What had the council put in the water? 'You're sure?' he asked with a smile. Nothing ever fazed this woman, certainly not her gammy leg, not a diabetic three-year-old, not a drunk for a husband.

'Yep, got all the usual signs. Thought I'd better let you know so I can get registered with Kat.'

Now, there was something that did tend to wind Jane up. Kat's attitude to her husband. Kat had tried to intervene one night at the pub when he'd been about to swing a fist at Jane. Something Flynn would've tried to prevent, too, if he'd been there. 'Kat's away at the moment so you'll get to meet Ally.' Of course, there were nine months to a pregnancy, and Kat was only away for one, but hopefully Ally could settle Jane into things so that she'd be happier with Kat this time round.

'Is she nice?' Jane's eyes lit up.

More than. 'You'll get along great guns. Now, I'm surmising that we need to discuss your arthritis meds for the duration of your pregnancy.'

The light in those eyes faded. She accepted her painful condition without a complaint, but she knew how hard the next few months were going to be. 'I've cut back already to what you've recommended before. There's no way I'm risking hurting junior in there.' Her hand did a circuit of her belly. 'Can't say I'm happy with the extra pain, but I want this wee one. Think I'll make it the last, though. Get my bits chopped out afterwards.'

As he made a note to that effect in her computer file, Flynn tried not to smile. Her bits. He got to hear all sorts of names for vaginas and

Fallopian tubes in this job. 'How far along do you think you are?'

'I've missed two periods. Should've come to see you sooner, I know, but that family of mine keeps me busy.' Jane wasn't mentioning the lack of money, but he knew about it. 'Anyway, it's not like I don't know what to expect. They haven't changed the way it's done in the last three years, have they?'

'Not that anyone's told me.'

After writing out prescriptions, ordering blood tests, including an HCG for confirmation of the pregnancy, and taking Jane's blood pressure, he took her along to meet Ally.

It wasn't until he was returning to his room and he passed Faye, who rolled her eyes at him, that he realised he was walking with a bounce in his stride and a smile on his face. All due to a certain midwife.

What was it about her that had him sitting up and taking notice? It had happened instantly. Right from that moment when Sheba had knocked her down and he'd reached out a hand to haul the dog off, only to be sidetracked by the most startling pair of hazel eyes he'd ever seen.

Whatever it was, he'd better put a lid on the sizzle before anyone else in the clinic started noticing. That was the last thing he needed, and no doubt Ally felt the same.

CHAPTER THREE

'FLYNN,' MEGAN CALLED from her office as he was shrugging into his jacket. 'The path lab's on line one.'

'Put them through.' Damn, he'd just seen Ally head out the front door for home. He'd intended talking to her before she left, maybe even walk with her as far as Kat's flat, then backtrack to home. Which, given he lived on the opposite side of town, showed how fried his brain had become in the last twenty-four hours.

For an instant he resented being a GP. There were never any moments just for him. Like it had been any different working as an emergency specialist. Yeah, but he'd chosen that career pathway, not had it forced on him. So he'd give up trying to raise Adam properly, hand him over to spend even more hours with day carers? No, he wouldn't. The disgruntled feeling disappeared in a flash, replaced with love. His little guy meant everything to him.

'Flynn?' Megan yelled. 'Get that, will you?'

He kicked the door shut and grabbed the persistently ringing phone from his desk. 'Flynn Reynolds. How can I help?' *Could you hurry up? I'm on a mission.*

'Doctor, this is Andrew from the lab. I'm calling about some biochemistry results on William Foster.'

William Foster, fifty-six and heading down the overweight path through too much alcohol and fatty food since his wife had died twelve months back. He'd complained of shoulder pain and general malaise so he'd ordered urgent tests to check what his heart might be up to. 'I'm listening.'

'His troponin's raised. As are his glucose and cholesterol. But it's the troponin I'm ringing about.'

He took down details of the abnormal results, even though Andrew would email them through within the next five minutes. Finding William's phone number, he was about to dial but thought better of it. Instead, he phoned Marie on the run. 'I'm going to be late.'

'I'll feed Adam dinner, then.'

Flynn sighed. 'I owe you. Again.'

Marie chuckled. 'Get over yourself. I love having him.'

Yeah, she did, but that didn't make everything right. For Adam. Or for him.

William lived ten minutes away and halfway there Flynn decided he should've rung first to make sure the man was at home and not at the club, enjoying a beer. William didn't know it yet, but beer would be off the menu for a while.

William opened his front door on the third knock, and appeared taken aback to find Flynn on his doorstep after dark. 'Doc, what's up?'

'Can I come in for a minute?'

William's eyes shifted sideways. 'What you want to tell me?'

The man was ominously pale. He hadn't been like that earlier. 'Let me in and we'll discuss it.' From the state of William's breathing and speech, Flynn knew there'd be a bottle of whisky on the bench. That wouldn't be helping the situation. 'It's important.'

With a sigh the older man stepped back, hauling the door wide at the same time. 'I haven't done the housework this week, Doc, so mind where you step.'

This week? Flynn tried not to breathe too deeply, and didn't bother looking into the rooms they passed. It was all too obvious the man was living in squalor. He wasn't coping with Edna's passing, hadn't since day one, and nothing Flynn or William's daughter had done or said made the slightest bit of difference. The man had given up, hence Flynn's visit. A phone call would never have worked. Besides, he needed to be with William as he absorbed the news.

In the kitchen William's shaky hands fidgeted with an empty glass he'd lifted from the table. He didn't look directly at Flynn, not even for a moment, but every few seconds his eyes darted sideways across the kitchen. Sure enough, an almost full whisky bottle was on the bench, as were three empty ones. How long had it taken for him to drink his way through those?

It would be too easy to tell the man some cold hard facts about his living conditions and his drinking, but Flynn couldn't do it. He understood totally what it was like to lose the woman he loved more than life. He suspected if it hadn't been for Adam and having to put on a brave face every single day, he might've made as big a mess of his own life after Anna had been killed. He still struggled with the sense of living a life mapped out by fate, one that held none of his choices.

Pulling out a chair, he indicated William should sit down. Then he straddled another one, not looking at the condition of the once beautiful brocade on the seat. 'William, your test results have come back. They're not good, I'm afraid.'

'Figured that'd be why you're here.'

'The major concern is that you've had a cardiac incident. A heart attack, William.'

Rheumy eyes lifted to stare at him, but William said nothing, just shrugged.

'You need to go to hospital tonight. They'll run more tests and keep an eye on you until they find the cause of the attack.'

'What else?' William wheezed the question.

'They'll give you advice on diet and exercise.'

Things he'd have no inclination to follow. The same as with any advice he had given him.

'I meant what other tests were bad?'

He was about to add to the man's gloomy outlook, but couldn't see a way around it. All he could hope for was that he shocked his patient into doing something about his lifestyle before it was too late. 'Your cholesterol's high, which probably explains your cardiac arrest. You've got diabetes and your liver's not in good nick.'

'I hit the jackpot, didn't I?' The sadness in William's voice told how much he didn't care any more. 'I don't suppose you went on a bender when you lost your wife, Doc.'

Yeah, he had. Just one huge bender, when he'd almost killed himself. Big enough and frightening enough to put him off ever doing it again. But he knew he still might've if it hadn't been for Adam. 'I couldn't afford to, William.'

'I get it. Your boy.'

'You've got family who care about you, too.' Flynn tried to think of something that might interest William in getting his act together, but nothing came to mind, apart from his daughter and grandkids. That had been tried before and William hadn't run with it. 'Now, don't get upset, but I've ordered the ambulance to transfer you to hospital. It should be here any minute.'

'I don't need that. I can drive myself there.'

'What if you have another heart attack and cause an accident that hurts someone?'

There was silence in the kitchen. Not a lot William could say to that. He was a decent man, unable to cope with a tragedy. He wasn't reckless with other people.

'I'll wait here until you're on your way. Want me to talk to your daughter?' Working in the ED, he'd have phoned the cardiologist and had William wheeled to the ward, no argument. Patients were in the ED because someone recognised the urgency of their situation. Urgent meant urgent—not talking and cajoling. He missed that fast pace at times, but if he got William under way to getting well then he'd feel deep satisfaction.

'After I've left. Don't want her telling me off tonight.' William stared around the kitchen, brought his gaze back to Flynn. 'Don't suppose I can have a whisky for the road.'

* * *

By the time Flynn finally made it home Adam was in his pyjamas and glued to the TV. 'Hiya, Dad.'

'Hello, my man.' Tonight he couldn't find it in him to make Adam stop watching—an Anna rule or not. Instead, he turned to Marie. 'I appreciate you bringing him home.'

Marie was already buttoning up her coat, the gaps between the buttons splayed wide over her baby bulge. 'Have you decided who's going to look after Adam when my little one arrives?' Marie was determined to look after Adam right up to the last minute. She'd also sorted through the numerous girls wanting to take her place until she was ready to take Adam back under her wing and had decided on two likely applicants.

'Caught. I'll get onto it.' He pushed his fingers through his hair. 'Tonight?'

'Whenever.' She laughed. 'It's not as though you'll be left high and dry. Half the island would love to look after Dr Reynolds's boy. Not just because he's such a cute little blighter either. There's a family likeness between father and son.'

'Haven't you got a husband waiting at home for his dinner?' He wasn't keen on dating any of the island's females. Too close to home and work. Anyway, no one had caught his interest in the last two years. Not until Ally had got knocked over by Sheba, that was.

Ally wasn't answering when he phoned after putting Adam to bed. She wasn't answering her phone when he called at nine, after giving in to the tiredness dragging at his bones and sitting down to watch a crime programme on TV. She might've answered if he'd rung as he was going to bed at ten thirty, but he didn't want her to think he was stalking her.

But she sure as hell stalked him right into bed. As he sprawled out under the covers he missed her not being there beside him, even though she'd never seen his bed, let alone lain in it. He stretched his legs wide to each side and got the same old empty spaces, only tonight they felt cold and lonely. Make that colder and lonelier. In his head, hot and sexy Ally with those brilliant hazel eyes was watching and laughing, teasing, playing with him. How was he supposed to remain aloof, for pity's sake? He was only human—last time he looked.

Was this what happened when he hadn't had sex for so long? Should he have been making an effort to find an obliging woman for a bit of relaxation and fun? He yawned.

Did Ally know she'd cranked up his libido? Yeah, it was quite possible she did, if the way the air crackled between them whenever they came within touching distance was any indication.

So follow up on it. Have some fun. Have sex. Have an affair with her. It would only be four weeks before Ally moved on. He wouldn't disrupt Adam's routine too much or for too long.

Flynn rolled over to punch his pillow and instead squashed his awakening reaction to the woman in his head. The air hissed out of his lungs as he grinned. That had to be a good sign for the future, didn't it?

'Morning, Ally,' Megan called as she stepped through the front door of the clinic on Tuesday. 'I see you've found the best coffee on the island already.'

'First thing I do on any job.' She sniffed the air appreciatively just to wind Megan up.

Scowling happily at her, Megan lifted her own container then asked, 'What did you think of the movie?'

'It was great. Nothing like a few vampires to fill in the evening.' She'd bumped into the receptionist and her boyfriend as they'd been walking into the theatre. 'Seeing you there made me feel I'd been living here for a while.'

Megan laughed. 'Small towns are like that. Believe me, people around here will know what you had for dinner last night.'

'Then they'll be giving me lectures on healthy eating. Fried chicken and chips from Mrs Chook's.' It had been delicious, even if she should've been looking for a salad bar. In winter? Hey, being good about food could sometimes be highly overrated. Anyway, she'd wanted comfort food because when she had gone back to the flat after work she'd felt unusually out of sorts. Arrival day in a new place, yes, that was normal; every other day thereafter, never.

This nomadic life had been one of her goals ever since she'd left school and become independent of the welfare system. Those goals had been simple—earn the money to put herself through a nursing degree then support herself entirely with a job that she could give everything to but which wouldn't tie her to one place. Along with that went to establish a life where she didn't depend on anyone for anything, including friendship or love.

So far it had worked out fine. Sure, there were the days when she wondered if she could risk getting close to someone. She had no experience of being loved, unconditionally or any other way, so the risks would be huge for everyone involved. She had enough painful memories of being moved on from one family to the next to prove how unworthy of being loved she was. At unsettled moments like this those memories underlined why she never intended taking a chance on finding someone to trust with her heart. Sometimes she wondered if her heart really was only there to pump blood.

In the midwife's room she dumped her bag and jacket, then wandered into the staffroom, surreptitiously on a mission to scope out Flynn, if he'd arrived. He must've, because suddenly her skin was warming up. Looking around the room, her eyes snagged with his where he sat on a chair balanced on two legs. She'd known he was there without seeing him. She'd felt an instant attraction before setting eyes on him. What was going on? Hadn't she just been remembering why she wasn't interested?

She took a gulp of coffee and spluttered as she burned her tongue. 'That's boiling.'

Concern replaced the heat in Flynn's gaze and the front legs of the chair banged onto the tiled floor as he came up onto his feet. 'You all right?' He snatched a paper towel off the roll on the wall. 'Here, spit it out.'

Taking the towel to wipe the dribble off her lips before he could, she muttered, 'Too late, I swallowed it instantly.' And could now feel it heating a track down her throat. 'I forget to take the lid off every time.' But usually she wasn't distracted enough to forget to sip first. 'Black coffee takes for ever to cool in these cardboard cups.'

'Slow learner, eh?' That smile should be banned. Or bottled. Or kissed.

It sent waves of heat expanding throughout her

body, unfurling a need so great she felt a tug of fear. What if she did give in to this almost over-whelming attraction? Could she walk away from it unscathed? Like she always did? This thing with Flynn didn't feel the same as her usual trysts. There was something between them she couldn't explain. But they wouldn't be getting started. Staying remote would keep things on an even keel. *You're not lovable. Forget that and you're toast.*

'I called you last night to ask how you felt about your first day here.'

So much for remote. He wasn't supposed to play friendly after hours. 'That explains one of two missed calls. I went to a movie and switched it off for the duration.'

Flynn looked awkward. 'I rang twice.'

'Did I miss something?' Had one of her patients gone into labour? Or developed prob-lems? Had Chrissie wanted to talk to her again? This wouldn't look good for her if she had.

'Relax. They were purely social calls.'

The way he drawled his words did everything but relax her. She managed through a dry mouth, 'That's all right, then.' Highly intelligent conversation going on here, but she was incapable of much more right now. He shouldn't be phoning her.

'Ally, I was wondering—'

'Morning, everyone.' Jerome strolled in. 'You came back for more, then, Ally?'

'Yes.' She shook her head to clear the heat haze. 'Missed the ferry back to the mainland so thought I'd fill in my day looking after your pregnant patients,' she joked pathetically.

Then Flynn asked, 'How was Chrissie when you talked to her after school?'

She wondered what he'd been going to ask before Jerome had interrupted. 'Resigned would best describe her attitude. But today might be a whole different story after a night thinking about it all.' Ally dropped onto a chair and stared her coffee. 'I hope she's going to be all right.' Chrissie still had to tell her mother. That'd be the toughest conversation of her young life.

'Like I said, Angela will be very supportive.' Flynn returned to his seat. 'Marie was happy with her new midwife, by the way.'

Marie was happy with her boss and his boy, with the impending birth of her baby, with her husband, with the whole world. 'I saw Adam for a few minutes when she came in. At least he'd stopped giggling.'

'Ah, you missed the standing in the dog's water bowl giggles, and the dollop of peanut butter on the floor right by Sheba's nose giggles.'

She could picture Adam now, bent over, howling with laughter. 'He's one very happy little boy, isn't he?'

Flynn's smile slipped. Oops. What had she gone and done? Sadness filtered into his eyes and she wanted to apologise with a hug for whatever she'd managed to stir up, but she didn't. Of course she didn't. Hugging a man she'd only met two days ago and who was one of her bosses wasn't the best idea she'd ever had. She sipped coffee instead—which perversely had turned lukewarm—and waited for the meeting to get under way.

'I see you had William admitted last night,' Faye said as she joined them.

Flynn looked relieved he'd been diverted from answering what she'd thought had been a harmless question. He hurried to explain. 'He'd had a cardiac event. Hardly surprising, given the way he's been living.'

'He'll be seen by a counsellor while in hospital. Maybe they can make him see reason,' Faye said. 'Not that we all haven't tried, I know.'

Flynn grimaced, his eyes still sad. 'I'm hoping this is the wake-up shock required to get him back on track.' He turned to Ally. 'William's wife succumbed to cancer last year.'

'That's terrible.' She shuddered. *See? Even if you got a good one, someone who never betrayed your trust, they still left you hurt and miserable.* No wonder Flynn looked sad. He seemed to hold all his patients dear.

Jerome spoke up. 'Ally, I believe you're doing house calls today. One of your patients is Matilda Livingstone. This is her first pregnancy. Be warned she's paranoid about something going wrong and will give you a million symptoms to sort through.'

Ally's interest perked up. 'Any particular reason for this behaviour?'

'She has a paranoid mother who suffered three miscarriages in her time and only carried one baby full term. She's fixated with making sure

Matilda checks everything again and again. It's almost as though she doesn't want her daughter to have a stress-free pregnancy.' Jerome shook his head, looking very puzzled.

'Mothers, eh?' She smiled, knowing her real thoughts about some mothers weren't showing. Ironic, considering she spent her days working with mums—the loving kind. 'Thanks for the nod. I'll tread carefully.'

'You know you've got the use of the clinic's car for your rounds, don't you?' Flynn asked.

'Sure do. I'm hoping it's a V8 supercharged car with wide tyres and a triple exhaust.'

'Red, of course.' Flynn grinned.

Faye stood up. 'Time to get the day cranking up. There seems to be a kindergarten lot of small children creating havoc in the waiting room.'

'Toby's doing vaccinations. For some reason, the mothers thought it better if they had them all done at the same time,' Jerome explained. 'Seems a bit much, considering that if one cries, they'll all cry.'

Flynn stood up. 'Who's going to cry when they've got Toby? That man's magic when it comes to jabbing a child.' He turned to Ally.

'I heard that you're also no slug when it comes to drawing bloods. Chrissie was seriously impressed, even told Toby that he needs practice.'

'So Toby's magic doesn't extend to older children?' Chrissie was still a child in many ways, baby on the way or not. When they'd talked about her HCG result yesterday afternoon it had been difficult. One minute Chrissie had acted all grown up and the next Ally could picture her tucked up with her teddy and a thumb in her mouth as she watched cartoons on TV.

'Sure it does, just not Chrissie. Has she mentioned when she might apprise her mother of the situation?'

'I think never would be her preferred approach. But realistically she's preparing herself. She did ask if I'd be present.'

'How do you feel about that?' Flynn asked.

'Of course I'll do it if that's what she wants, but I'd have thought you, as the family doctor, should be the one to talk to Angela with her.'

Flynn didn't look fazed. 'If she's relaxed with you then that's good. I'm not getting on my high horse because she's my patient. What works for her works for me. Or we can both be there.'

'Thanks.' Why was she thanking him? Shrugging, she added, 'Guess I'd better get on the road. My first appointment's at nine and I haven't looked at the map yet.'

Flynn gave her that devastating smile of his. 'You're not in Melbourne now. Come here and tell me who you're visiting.' He closed the door behind Jerome and Ally felt as though the air had been sucked out of the room.

What was he doing? Here? At work? Any minute someone could walk in for a coffee.

'Here's the clinic.' Flynn tapped his finger on the back of the door. 'Who's first on your list?'

Ally's face reddened as her gaze took in the map pinned to the door. 'Um.' Think, damn it, peanut brain. 'Erika Teale.'

She watched in fascination as Flynn's finger swept across the map and stopped to tap at some point that made no sense whatsoever. Running her tongue over her lips, she tried to sound sane and sensible. 'That's next to the golf ranch.' Too squeaky, but at least she'd got something out.

He turned to stare at her. 'Are you all right? Is map-reading not your forte?'

'I'm better with drawing bloods.' No one could read a map when Flynn was less than two feet away. Even a simple map like this one suddenly became too complex. Taking a step closer to the map—and Flynn—she leaned forwards to study the roads leading to Erika's house. Truth was, despite moving from town to town every few weeks she'd never got the hang of maps. 'So which side of the golf place is she on?' Why did he have to smell so yummy?

'What are you doing tonight?'

Gulp. Nothing. Why? 'Eating food and washing dirty clothes.' Like there was a lot of those, but she had to sound busy. Saying 'Nothing' was pathetic.

'Have dinner with me. We could go to the Italian café. It's simple but the food's delicious.'

She gasped. *Yes*, her head screamed. *I'd love to. Yes, yes, yes.* 'No, thanks,' came from her mouth. Sanity had prevailed. Just. 'You're married.'

Flynn's mouth flattened, and his thumb on his right hand flicked the tell-tale gold band round and round on his finger. The light went out in his eyes. 'I'm a widower. My wife died two years back.'

Her shoulders dropped their indignant stance as his words sank in. 'Oh.' She was getting good at these inane comments. 'I'm so sorry. That must be difficult for you and Adam. But he seems so happy, you must be a great father.'

Shut up, dribble mouth.

But he's free, available.

Yeah. I'm a cow.

Guilt followed and she reached a hand to his arm, touched him lightly. 'I don't know what else to say. How do you manage?' The way he looked at that moment, he'd be retracting his invitation any second.

'Adam keeps me sane and on the straight and narrow. If it wasn't for him, who knows what I might've done at the time?' Sadness flicked across his face and then he looked directly at her and banished it with a smile. 'For the record, you're the first woman I've asked on a date in the last two years. The only woman I've looked at twice and even considered taking out.' Then his smile faltered. 'I guess it's not much of an offer, going to the Italian café, considering what you must be used to in the city.'

'Flynn, it's not about where I go but who I go with. I'd love to try the local Italian with you.' She meant every word. A wave of excitement rolled through her. A date—with this man—who set her trembling just by looking at her. What more could she want? Bring it on.

'Then I'll pick you up after I've put Adam to bed and got the babysitter settled. Probably near eight, if that's all right?' There was relief and excitement mingling in his expression, in those cobalt eyes locked on her, in the way he stood tall.

She was struggling to keep up with all his emotions. 'Perfect.' She'd have time for a shower, to wash and blow-dry her hair, apply new make-up and generally tart herself up. Bring it on, she repeated silently.

CHAPTER FOUR

SOMEONE SHOULD'VE TOLD the pregnancy gods that Ally had a date and needed at the minimum an hour to get ready. Seems that memo had never gone out.

As she slammed through the front door of the flat at seven forty-five, Ally was cursing, fit to turn the air blue. 'Babies, love their wee souls, need to learn right from the get-go to hold off interrupting the well-laid plans of their midwife.'

Baby Hill thought cranking up his mum's blood pressure and making her ankles swell was a fun thing to do a couple of weeks out from his arrival. Pre-eclampsia ran through Vicky Hill's family but she'd been distressed about having to go to hospital for an evaluation, and it had taken a while to calm her down. Jerome had finally talked to his patient and managed to get her on her way with her thankfully calm husband.

Ally suspected some of Vicky's worry was

because she was dealing with a new midwife right on the day she needed Kat to be there for her. Ally had no problem with that. Being a midwife had a lot to do with good relationships and they weren't formed easily with her, due to the come-and-go nature of her locum job.

The shower hadn't even fully warmed up when Ally leapt under the water. Goose bumps rose on her skin. Washing her hair was off the list. A hard brush to remove the kinks from the tie that kept it back all day would suffice. If there was time. She'd make time. After slipping on a black G-string, she snatched up a pair of black, body-hugging jeans to wriggle her way into. The lace push-up bra did wonders for her breasts and gave a great line to the red merino top she tugged over her head.

The doorbell rang as she picked up the mascara wand. Flick, flick. Then a faster-than-planned brush of her hair and she was as ready as she was ever going to be.

She might not have had all the time she'd wanted, but by the look on Flynn's face she hadn't done too badly. His Adam's apple bobbed as his gaze cruised the length of her, making her feel happy with the hurried result.

'Let's go,' he croaked.

We could stay here and not bother with dinner. Or we can do both.

She slammed the front door shut behind her and stepped down the path. 'I'm starving.' For food. For man. For fun.

Flynn knew he should look away. Now. But how? His head had locked into place so that he stared at this amazing woman seated opposite him in the small cubicle they'd been shown to by the waiter. He hadn't seen her with her hair down before. Shining light brown hair gleaming in the light from wall sconces beside their table and setting his body on fire. He desperately wanted to run his hands through those silky layers, and over it, and underneath at the back of her neck.

'Excuse me, Dr Reynolds. Would you like to order wine with your meal?'

Caught. Staring at his lady friend. Reluctantly looking up, he saw one of his young patients holding out the wine menu. 'Hello, Jordan.

How's the rugby going? Got a game this week-end?' He glanced down the blurred list of wines.

'It's high school reps this weekend. We're going up to Melbourne on Thursday.'

After checking with Ally about what she pre-ferred, he ordered a bottle of Merlot, and told Jordan what meals they'd chosen. Then he leaned back and returned his attention to Ally, finding her watching him with a little smile curving that inviting mouth.

'How often do you get out like this?' she asked.

'Never. When I go out it's usually with people from work.' Comfortable but not exhilarating.

'Who's looking after Adam tonight? Not Marie?'

'No, she needs her baby sleep. Jerome's daugh-ter came round, bringing her homework with her.' Better than having a boyfriend tag along, like the last girl he'd used when he'd had a meet-ing to attend. He'd sacked her because of that boyfriend distracting her so she hadn't heard Adam crying.

'So they know at work that you and I are out together?' Her eyes widened with caution.

'There's no point trying to be discreet on Phillip Island. Everyone knows everyone's business all too quickly, even if you try to hide it.'

The tip of her tongue licked the centre point of her top lip. In, out, in, out.

Flynn suppressed a groan and tried to ignore the flare of need unfurling low down. What was it about this woman compared to any of the other hundreds he'd crossed paths with over the last two years that had him wanting her so much? Admittedly, for a good part of those years he'd been wound up in grief and guilt so, of course, he hadn't been the slightest bit interested. His libido hadn't been tweaked once. Yet in walks Ally Parker and, slam-bang, he could no longer think straight.

The owner of the café brought their wine over and with a flourish poured a glass for Ally. '*Signorina*, welcome to the island. I am Giuseppe and this is my café. I am glad our favourite doctor has brought you here to enjoy our food.'

Ally raised her glass to Giuseppe. 'Thank you for your welcome. Is everyone on Phillip Island as kind as you and the medical centre staff?'

'*Si*, everyone. You've come at the right time of

year when there are very few tourists. Summer is much busier and no time for the small chat.'

Finally Giuseppe got around to filling Flynn's glass, and gave him a surreptitious wink as he set the bottle on the table. 'Enjoy your evening, Doctor.'

Cheeky old man. Flynn grinned despite himself. 'I intend to.'

Ally watched him walk away, a smile lighting her pretty face. 'I could get to like this.' Then the smile slipped. 'But only for a month. Then I'll have somewhere else nice and friendly to visit while I relieve yet another midwife.'

He wanted to ask what compelled her to only take short-term contracts, but as he opened his mouth the thought of possibly spoiling what was potentially going to be a wonderful evening had him shutting up fast. Then their meals arrived and all questions evaporated in the hot scent of garlic and cream and tomatoes wafting between them.

Ally sighed as she gazed at her dish. 'Now, that looks like the perfect carbonara.' This time her tongue slid across first her bottom lip and then the top one. What else could she do with that tongue? Lifting her eyes, she studied his pizza. 'That looks delicious, too.'

'I know it will be.' The best pizzas he'd ever tasted had been made right here. 'One day I'll get to trying a pasta dish, but I can't get past the pizzas.'

Sipping her wine, Ally smiled directly at him. 'Thank you for bringing me here.'

'It's the best idea I've had in a long time.' Had he really just said that? Yes, and why not? It was only the truth. Picking up a wedge of pizza, he held it out to her. 'Try that.'

Her teeth were white and perfect. She bit into the wedge and sat back to savour the flavours of tomato and basil that would be exploding in her mouth. As he watched her enjoyment, he took a bite. Ally closed her eyes and smiled as she chewed. 'How do you do that?' he asked.

She swallowed and her eyelids lifted. 'Here, you must try this.' She twirled her fork in her pasta and leaned close to place it in his mouth.

The scent of hot food and Ally mingled, teasing him as he took her offering. The tastes of bacon and cream burst across his tongue.

'Divine.' Though he suspected cardboard would taste just as good right now.

They shared another wedge of pizza. Then Ally put her hands around her plate. 'Not sharing any more.'

Moments later she raised her glass to smile over the rim at him and let those sultry eyes study him.

Flynn sneaked his fork onto her plate and helped himself. 'You think you're keeping this to yourself?' Not that his stomach was in the mood for more food while she was looking at him like he was sexy. He felt alive and on top of his game, very different from his usual sad and exhausted state.

Her tongue ran around the edge of her glass, sending desire firing through his body heading straight for his manhood. *Pow.* 'You're flirting with me, Miss Ally.'

'Yes.' Her tongue lapped at her wine, sending his hormones into overdrive.

He placed the fork, still laden with carbonara, on his plate. 'Come here,' he growled. 'I've wanted to do this for two whole days.'

He placed his fingers on her cheeks to draw

her closer. Pressing his mouth to her lips, all he was aware of was this amazing woman and the taste, the feel, the heat of her.

Finally, some time later—minutes or hours?— Flynn led Ally outside, only vaguely aware they'd eaten tiramisu for dessert, and hoped he'd had enough smarts to pay the bill before leaving. No worry, Giuseppe knew where to find him. In one hand he held the wine bottle, still half-full, while his other arm wrapped around Ally's waist as she leaned in close, her head on his shoulder, her arm around him with her hand in his pocket, stroking his hip, stroking, stroking.

Forget the car. He led her across the road and down to the beach. It was cold, but he was hot. They didn't talk, and the moment they were out of sight of the few people out on the road, Ally turned into him, pressing her body hard against his. Her hands linked at the back of his neck and she tugged his mouth down to hers.

The bottle dropped to the sand as he slid his hands under her top. Her skin was satin, hot satin. Splaying his fingers, he smoothed his hands back and forth, touching more of her, while his mouth tasted her, his tongue dancing around hers. He wanted her. Now.

'Ally?' he managed to groan out between kisses.

Between their crushed-together bodies she slipped a hand to his trousers, tugged his zip down. The breath caught in his throat as her fingers wrapped around him.

'Ally.' This time there was no question in his mind.

She rubbed him, up, down. Up, down.

Reaching for her jeans, he pushed and pulled until he had access to her, trying—and nearly failing—to remain focused on giving her pleasure. She was wet to his touch, moaning as his fingers touched her, and she came almost instantly, crying out as she rocked against his hand. Her hand squeezed him, eased, squeezed again, and his release came quickly.

Too quickly. 'Can we do that again?' he murmured against that soft hair.

Ally had wrapped herself against him, her arms under his jacket, her breaths sharp against his chest. Her head moved up and down. 'Definitely.'

'Come on, we'll go home.'

Her head lifted. 'You've got a babysitter. We could go to the flat.'

His lips traced a kiss across her forehead and down her cheek. 'Are you always so sensible?' He'd fried any brain matter he had. 'Good thinking.'

'What are we waiting for?' Ally spun around and took his hand to drag him back up the beach to his car.

The flat was less than five minutes away. Thank goodness. He didn't know how he'd manage to keep two hands on the steering wheel for that long, let alone actually function well enough to drive.

The moment she shut the front door behind them Ally grabbed Flynn's hand and almost ran to the bedroom. That had been amazing on the beach, but it was only a taste of what she knew they could have. It had been nowhere near enough.

She laughed out loud. 'I want to wrap myself around you.' She began tearing clothes off. Flynn's and hers. 'I want to get naked and up close with you.'

'Stop.' It was a command.

And she obeyed. 'Yes?'

'Those knickers. Don't take them off. Not yet.'

So he was into G-strings. She turned and saucily moved her derrière, then slowly lifted her top up to her breasts, oh, so slowly over them, and finally above her head, tossing it into the corner.

Then turned around, reaching behind her to unclasp her bra. Flynn's eyes followed every move. When she shrugged out of the lace creation, his hands rose to her breasts, ever so lightly brushing across her nipples and sending swirls of need zipping through her. Once had definitely not been enough with this man.

Twice probably wouldn't be, either. This was already cranking up to be a fling of monumental proportions. Her time on Phillip Island had just got a whole lot more interesting and exciting.

'Flynn.' His name fell as a groan between them.

As he leaned over to take her nipple in his mouth he smiled. A smile full of wonder and longing. A smile that wound around her heart.

Back off. Now. Your heart never gets involved. Back off. Remember who, what you are. A nomad, soon to be on the road again. Remember. You take no passengers.

Flynn softly bit her breast, sending rationale out the window. Her hands gripped his head to keep his mouth exactly where it was. His hands cupped her backside. Tipping her head back so her hair fell down her back, Ally went with the overwhelming need crawling through her, filling every place, warming every muscle until she quivered with such desire she thought she'd explode.

Flynn's mouth traced kisses up her throat, then began a long, exploratory trip downward. Back to her breasts, then her stomach and beyond. It was impossible to keep up with him, to savour each and every stroke. They all melted into one, and when her legs trembled so much she could barely stand, Flynn gently guided her onto the bed, where he joined her, his erection throbbing when she placed her hand around him and brought him to where she throbbed for him.

Ally rolled over and groaned. *Is there any part of me that doesn't ache?* A delicious, morning-after-mind-blowing-sex ache that pulled the energy out of her and left her feeling relaxed and unwilling to get up to face the day.

She was expected at work by eight thirty. *Yeah, tell that to someone who cares.* But she dragged herself upright and stared around. The bed was a shambles, with the sheets twisted, the cover skew-whiff and the pillows on the floor.

What a night. Really only for an hour, but for once she doubted she could've gone all night. Not with Flynn. He took it out of her, he was so good.

The phone rang. It wasn't on her bedside table or on the floor next to the bed. But it did sound as though it was in this room. She tossed the cover aside, shivering as winter air hit her bare skin. Lifting the sheets and pillows, she found her jeans, but not what she was looking for. 'Don't hang up.' What if it was one of her mothers having contractions? 'Where is the blasted phone?'

Picking up her top from the corner where she'd thrown it last night, she pounced, pressed the phone's green button. 'Morning, Ally Parker speaking.'

'Morning, gorgeous,' Flynn's voice drawled

in her ear. 'Thought I'd make sure you're wide-awake.'

'And if I hadn't been?' The concern backed off a notch at the sound of his warm tone. 'You'd have come around and hauled me out of bed?'

'My oath I would.'

'That does it. I'm sound asleep.' What was wrong with her? Encouraging Flynn was not the way to go.

His laugh filled her with happiness. 'Unfortunately I have a certain small individual with me this morning and I know he'd love nothing better than to try and pull you out of bed.'

'So not a good look, considering I'm naked.' She'd left her brain on the beach. Had to have.

Flynn growled. 'I certainly wouldn't be able to fault that.'

Then she saw the time. 'Is it really eight o'clock? It can't be. Got to go. I'm going to be late.' She hung up before he could say anything else and ran for the bathroom. The left side of her left brain argued with the right side about what she was doing with Flynn.

'Only five minutes late,' she gasped, as she charged into the staffroom. A large coffee in a takeout mug stood on the table at the spot where she usually sat. 'Black and strong,' Flynn muttered, as he joined her.

'You're wonderful.' She popped the lid off.

Jerome and Toby sauntered in. 'What did you think of our local Italian?' Jerome asked with a twinkle in his eye.

'I'm hooked. Definitely going back there again.' Her knee nudged Flynn's under the table.

He pushed back as he continued to stare across at the other men. 'She's got Giuseppe eating out of her hand.'

I thought that was your hand. 'He's a sweetheart.'

'Ally.' Megan popped her head around the door. 'You've got visitors. Chrissie and her mum.'

Back to earth with a thud. Reality kicked in. 'Showtime.' Ally stood up, sipped her coffee, found it cool enough to gulp some down. No way could she start her day without her fix, especially not this morning. Her stomach was complaining about the lack of breakfast, but it'd have to make do with caffeine. 'Is it okay if I go and see Chrissie? Or would you prefer I stay for the meeting?'

'Don't worry about the meeting. One of us can fill you in later if there's anything you need to know,' Toby told her.

Flynn spoke up. 'If you need me, just call. But I'm sure you'll be fine.'

'Chrissie's mum would have to be dense not to know why her daughter has requested an appointment with a midwife, wouldn't she?'

Flynn nodded. 'And dense is not a word I'd use to describe Angela. She's probably cottoned on but could be denying it.'

Angela didn't deny it for any longer than it took for the three of them to be seated in Ally's room with the door firmly shut. 'You're going to tell me Chrissie's pregnant, aren't you?'

'Actually, I was hoping Chrissie might've told you.' She looked at the girl and found nothing but despair blinking out at her. Dark shadows lined the skin beneath her sad eyes and her mouth was turned downwards, while her hands fidgeted on her thighs. 'Chrissie, did you get any sleep last night?'

She shook her head. 'I was thinking, you know? About everything.' Her shoulders dropped even lower. 'I'm sorry, Mum. I didn't mean it to happen.'

'Now, that I can understand.' Angela might have been expecting the news but she still looked shocked. 'All too well.' She breathed deeply, her chest rising. 'How far along are you, do you know?' Her gaze shifted from her daughter to Ally and then back to Chrissie.

'Nearly twelve weeks.' Chrissie's voice was little more than a whisper. 'You're disappointed in me, aren't you?'

Angela sat ramrod straight. Her hands were clenched together, but her eyes were soft and there was gentleness in her next words. 'No, sweetheart, I think you're the one who's going to be disappointed. You had so many plans for your future and none of them included a baby.'

'But you managed. You've got a good job. You're the best mum ever.'

'Chrissie, love.' Angela sniffed, and reached for one of her daughter's hands. 'A good job, yes, but not the career I'd planned on.'

Ally stood up and crossed to the window to give them some space. They didn't need her there. Yet. Flynn had been right. This woman was a good mum. *Why didn't I have one like her? Why didn't I have one at all? One who loved me from the day I was born?*

Behind her the conversation became erratic as Chrissie and Angela worked their way through the minefield they were facing. At least they were facing it together.

'Do you regret having me?' Chrissie squeaked.

'Never.' A chair scratched over the surface of the floor and when Ally took a quick peek she saw Angela holding her daughter in her arms. 'Never, ever. Not for one minute.'

'I'm keeping my baby, Mum.'

Ally held her breath. This was the moment when Angela might finally crack. She fully understood the pitfalls of single parenthood. And the joys. But she'd want more for Chrissie.

Angela was strong. 'I thought you'd say that. I hope your child will love its grandmother as much as you loved your grandfather, my girl, because we're in this together. Understand?'

As Chrissie burst into long-overdue tears, Ally sneaked out the door, closing it softly behind her. In the storeroom she wiped her own eyes.

Did that girl understand how loved she was? How lucky?

'Hey, don't tell me it was that bad in there.' Flynn stood before her, holding the box of tissues she'd been groping for.

'It was beautiful.' Blow. 'What an amazing mother Angela is. Chrissie will be, too, if that's the example she's got to follow.'

'Told you.' Did he have to sound so pleased with himself? His finger tipped her chin up so she had to meet his kind gaze. 'Come and finish that coffee I bought you. We can zap it in the microwave.'

He'd be thinking she was a right idiot, hiding in the cupboard, crying, because her patient had just told her mother she was pregnant. 'I'll give them five minutes and then go and discuss pregnancy care and health.'

'Make it ten. You'll be feeling better and they'll have run out of things to say to each other for a while.' His hand on her elbow felt so right. And for the first time it wasn't about heat and desire but warmth and care.

More stupid tears spurted from her eyes. Her third day here and he was being gentle and kind to her. Right now she liked this new scenario. Thank goodness Flynn would think these fresh tears were more of the same—all about Chrissie and her mother, not about him. And her.

CHAPTER FIVE

THE MOMENT FLYNN saw the clinic's car turn into the parking lot on Friday night he couldn't hold back a smile. A smile for no other reason than he was glad to see Ally. Her image was pinned up in his skull like a photo on a notice-board. More than one photo. There was the one of Ally in those leg-hugging, butt-defining jeans and the red jersey that accentuated her breasts. Then the other: a naked version showing those shapely legs, slim hips and delicious breasts.

There was a third: tearful Ally, hiding away and looking lost and lonely. What was that about?

The front door crashed against the wall as she elbowed it wide and carried her bag in. 'Hi, Flynn, you're working late. Had an emergency?'

Yep, two hours without laying eyes on you definitely constitutes an emergency. 'Do you want to join Adam and me for dinner? There's a chicken casserole cooking as we speak. Nothing flash, but it should be tasty.'

'A casserole's not flash?' Her smile warmed him right down to his toes. 'My mouth's watering already.'

'Is that a yes, then?' His lungs stopped functioning as he waited for her reply.

'Are you sure there'll be enough?' As he was about to answer in the affirmative, she asked, 'Shall I stop in at the supermarket and get some garlic bread to go with the meal? Some wine?'

'Good idea. I left the Merlot behind the other night. On the beach,' he added with a grin.

'You're too easily distracted, that's your problem.' Her mouth stretched into a return smile. 'Someone probably got lucky when they went for a walk that morning.'

A devilish look crossed his face and his eyes widened. 'I got lucky that night.'

'A dinner invitation will get me every time.' She swatted his arm. 'What's your address? Better give me precise directions if you really want me to join you.'

'The island's not too large and most people

know where to find me.' Glancing at his watch, he added, 'I'll get home so Marie can leave.'

Flynn hummed all the way home, something he hadn't done in for ever. Even without Tuesday night's sexual encounters, the fact that Ally was coming to his place for a meal made him feel good. Mealtimes weren't lonely because Adam was there, but sometimes he wished for adult conversation while he enjoyed his dinner. He'd also like an occasional break from Adam's usual grizzles about what he was being made to eat. His boy was a picky eater. Just because his mother had wanted him to eat well, it didn't mean Adam agreed.

Flynn shook his head. Where did Adam come into this? This hyper mood had nothing to do with him. Try Ally. And himself. *Be honest, admit you want a repeat of Tuesday night's sex.*

Guilt hit hard and fast.

What was he thinking? How could he be having fun when Anna was gone? He didn't deserve to. It had been his fault she hadn't been happy with her life. He should've taken the time to listen to her when she'd tried to explain why it was so important to her to leave the city behind.

He'd loved his life in Melbourne, had thought he was well on the way to making a big name for himself in emergency medicine. Sure, he hadn't always been there for Anna and Adam, had missed meals and some firsts, like Adam saying 'Hello, Mummy', but they'd agreed before Adam had been conceived that he'd be working long hours, getting established, and that it would take a few years before he backed off so they could enjoy the lifestyle they both had wanted.

Anna had quickly forgotten their agreement once Adam had arrived, instead becoming more demanding for him to give up his aspirations and move to family-orientated Phillip Island. What he hadn't told Anna before she'd died was that he'd begun talks with the head of the ED to cut down his hours. It would've been a compromise. Too late. Anna had driven into an oncoming tram, and he and Adam had moved to her island full-time. Sometimes he had regrets about that—regrets that filled him with guilt. This was right for Adam. He should've done it for Anna while he could.

Turning into his drive, he automatically pressed

the garage door opener and drove in, hauled on the handbrake and switched off the engine. He tipped his head back against the headrest. 'Anna, I miss you.'

A lone tear tracked down his cheek.

Is it wrong to want to have some fun? To want to move on and forge a new life for me and our boy? Adam misses his mummy so much I'm afraid I'm getting it all wrong. I try to do things as you'd want, but sometimes I feel I'm living your life, not mine.

The engine creaked as it began cooling down. Sheba nudged her wet nose against his window and Flynn dragged himself out of the car. He didn't have time to sit around feeling sorry for himself. Rightly or wrongly, Ally was coming to dinner.

After stopping off at the supermarket, Ally went back to the flat and had a quick shower, before changing into jeans and a clean shirt. She took a moment to brush her ponytail out, letting it fall onto her shoulders. If the way Flynn kept running his hands through it the other night was an indicator, he obviously liked her hair.

She checked her phone for texts. Nothing. Not even from Darcie. She quickly texted.

How's things?

The reply was instant.

The usual. What r u doing 2night?

Having dinner with hot man.

You're not wasting time.

Did I mention his 4-yr-old son?

Ally? That's different for you.

Ally slipped her phone into her pocket without answering. What could she say? In one short message Darcie had underlined her unease.

Swiping mascara over her lashes, she stared at her reflection in the mirror. Most of the day, even when busy with patients, a sense of restlessness had dogged her. Strange. Her first-day nerves weren't going away.

Get over it. Coming to a new job's nothing like starting over with a new family when you're scared and wondering if they'll love you enough to keep you past the end of the first week. Don't let the worry bugs tip you off track. You're in control these days.

She twisted the mascara stick into its holder so hard it snapped.

Thank goodness she had something to do tonight other than sit alone in that pokey lounge, eating takeaways and watching something boring on TV. She'd be with Flynn and his boy, and be able to have a conversation. What about didn't matter, as long as she had company for a few hours. It would be an added bonus if she and Flynn ended up in bed. But she wasn't sure if it would happen, with Adam being in the house, Flynn rightly being super-protective of him.

Then she laughed at herself. Since when did she put sex second to conversation? After one night with Flynn she hadn't stopped wondering where he'd been all her life. What was happening? Had her regular hormones packed their bags and taken a hike, only to be replaced with a needier version?

She froze, stared into the mirror, found only the same face she'd been covering with make-up for years. No drastic changes had occurred.

The same old wariness mixed with a don't-mess-with-me glint blinked out of her eyes. And behind that the one emotion she hoped no one ever saw—her need to be loved.

Dropping her head, she planted her hands wide on the bathroom counter, stared into the basin and concentrated on forcing that old, childish yearning away.

Sex with Flynn and now this? Why now? Here? What was it about him that had the locks turning on her tightly sealed box of needs and longings?

She couldn't visit him. Throwing the mascara wand at the bin, she grimaced. She had to, then she'd see that he was just an everyday man working to raise his son and not someone to get in a stew over. If he was wise he'd never want a woman as mixed up as her in Adam's life.

A quick glance in the mirror and she dredged up a smile.

Attagirl. You're doing good. She kissed her fingertips and waved them at her image. But right now she'd love a hug.

Ally got her hug within seconds of stepping inside Flynn's house.

'Hey, there.' His eyes were sombre and his mouth not smiling as he wrapped her in his arms. Her cheek automatically nestled against his chest. Her determination to be Ally the aloof midwife wobbled. *Should've stayed away. At least until this weird phase passes.*

Then Adam leapt at her, nearly knocking her off her feet and winding his arms around her waist.

'Is this a family thing?' she asked, as she staggered back against the wall. She dredged up a smile for Adam.

'Easy, Adam, not so hard. You're hurting Ally.'

'No, I'm not,' he answered. Then he was racing down the hall to where light spilled from a room. 'Now we can eat.'

'There's an honest welcome.' Kind of heartwarming. 'I'm sorry if I've kept you waiting.'

Flynn shook his head. 'You're not late. You could've got here by midday and Adam would've been waiting for dinner. He's a bottomless pit when it comes to his favourite food.'

'I bought him a wee treat at the supermarket. I hope that's all right.' The house was abnormally quiet. No blaring TV, she realised.

'The occasional one's fine, but I try not to spoil him with too much sugar and fatty foods. His mother held strong beliefs about giving children the right foods early on to establish a good lifestyle for growing up healthy. Healthy body, healthy mind was a saying close to her heart.'

He was trying to implement his late wife's beliefs. 'Fair enough.' Ally had no idea what it must be like to be suddenly left as a solo parent to a two-year-old, especially while juggling a demanding career. 'Have you always worked on Phillip Island?'

'Only since Anna died.' Flynn found matching glasses and poured the Chardonnay she'd brought. 'I was an emergency consultant in Melbourne. Being a GP is relatively new for me, and vastly different from my previous life.'

'So you had to re-specialise?' Why the drastic change?

'It was a formality really as my specialty leant itself to general practice.' He lifted his glass and tapped the rim to hers. 'Cheers. Thanks for this.'

The wine was delicious, and from the way Flynn's mouth finally tipped up into a smile after he'd tasted it, he thought so, too.

'Thanks for feeding me.' She pulled out a bar stool from under the bench and arranged herself on it to watch Flynn put the finishing touches to dinner. *Looking for the everyday man?*

As he chopped parsley he continued the conversation in a more relaxed tone. 'Anna grew up here and it had always been her intention to return once she had a family.' His finger slid along the flat of the knife to remove tiny pieces of the herb and add them to the small pile he'd created. 'I wasn't ready to give up my career in the city. I was doing well, making a name for myself, working every hour available and more. We lived in a big house in the right suburb, had Adam registered for the best schools before he was born. It was the life *I'd* dreamed of having.'

She sensed a deep well of sadness in Flynn as he sprinkled the parsley on the casserole and rinsed his hands under the tap. *Not quite the definition of an everyday man.* Hadn't he and Anna discussed where they wanted to live and work before they'd married? Before they'd started a family? 'Yet here you are, everyone's favourite GP, living in a quiet suburban neighbourhood, seemingly quite happy with it all. Apart from what happened to your wife, of course,' she added hurriedly.

She wanted to know more about him, his past, his plans for the future. She craved more than to share some nights in bed with him. *Leave. Now.* But her butt remained firmly on the seat and her feet tucked under the stool. She'd have to stay and work through whatever was ailing her.

Flynn's smile was wry. 'Odd how it turned out. It took Anna's death for me to wake up to what was important. Family is everything, and Adam is my family, so here we are.' He held cutlery out for her to take across to the table.

Did he add under his breath, 'Living the life Anna wanted for all of us?' If he did, then he'd pull the shutters down on any kind of relationship other than a fling. His late wife wouldn't be wanting him to have a woman flitting in and out of his life, and definitely not Adam's.

Relief was instant. She didn't have to fight this sense of wanting more from him. There wasn't going to be anything other than sex and a meal or two. *You're jumping the gun. He mightn't even want the sex part any more.* Except when she glanced across to where he was dishing up the meal, she knew he did. It was there in the way he watched her, not taking a blind bit of notice where he spooned chicken and gravy. When their gazes locked she was instantly transported back to the moment they'd come together on the beach. Oh, yes, there were going to be more bed games.

Games that didn't involve her heart and soul, just her hormones and body.

'What is there to do on the island during winter?' Apart from going to bed with sexy doctors. 'I read somewhere about a racetrack, but there's not going to be a race meeting this month.'

'Do you like watching cars going round and round for hours on end?' He looked bored just thinking about it.

'I've never been, but I'm always looking for new adventures.'

'So what do you do with your spare time?'

Not a lot. Her standard time-fillers were, 'Shopping, movies, sunbathing on the beach, swimming, listening to music.'

'That's it?' His eyebrows lifted. 'Seriously?'

'What's wrong with that? It's plenty.' *I don't have a child to look after. Or a house to clean and maintain. Or a partner who wants me to follow him around.*

Flynn shook his head. 'Don't tell me your life is all work and no play?'

She locked her eyes on him. 'No play? Care to rephrase that?' She'd done playing the other night—with him.

He grinned. 'How about we take you to see the penguins this weekend? It's something I can take Adam to with us.'

'Penguins?' Adam's head swivelled round so fast he should've got an instant headache.

'Big Ears always hears certain words.' Flynn shrugged.

'Can we really go, Dad? They're funny, Ally.' Adam leapt up from the table to do his best impersonation of a penguin, and Sheba got up to run circles around him. Next Adam was having a fit of giggles.

Ally chuckled. 'I love it when he does that. Okay, yes, let's go and see these creatures.' It would be something to look forward to. Going out with an everyday man and his child. Different from her usual pursuits. She bobbed her head at Adam and held her arms tightly by her sides as she shuffled across the floor.

Adam rewarded her with more giggles as they returned to the table.

'That's enough, you two.' Flynn looked so much better when he laughed. 'Sorry we're eating early, but Adam needs to have his bath and get to bed.' Flynn didn't look sorry at all.

'I understand you must have a routine. Don't ever think you have to change it for me. I'm more than happy being fed,' she said, before forking up a mouthful of chicken. 'This is better than anything I'd make, believe me.'

Adam pushed his plate aside. 'Are we having pudding, Dad?'

'I've chopped up some oranges and kiwi fruit. Just need to add the banana when we're ready.'

'Can I get the ice cream out of the freezer?'

'Yes, you can tonight since we've got a visitor.' Flynn winked at her. 'You'll get an invitation every day now.'

I wish. 'I'll clean up the kitchen after dinner.' A small price for a home-cooked meal.

While Flynn was putting Adam to bed, Ally cleared away the plates. Once she'd put the last pot into the dishwasher and wiped down the benches she approached the coffee machine and began preparing two cappuccinos. 'These things make decent frothy milk,' she commented as Flynn joined her. 'How's Adam?'

'Asleep, thank goodness.' He took the coffees over to the lounge.

Following, she asked, 'This your quiet time?'

'Definitely. Don't get me wrong, I love my boy, but to have a couple of hours to unwind from the day before I go to bed is bliss.'

Bed. There it was. The place she wanted to be with Flynn right now. But he'd sat down and was stretching his legs out in front of him. She remembered those legs with no clothing to hide the muscles or keep her hands off his skin. Skin that covered more muscle and hot body the farther up she trailed her gaze. *Stop it.* She sipped the coffee, gasped as it burned her tongue. 'I'm such a slow learner.'

He stood up to take the mug out of her hand and place it on a small table beside the chair. Then he reached for her hands and pulled her to her feet. His mouth was on hers in an instant; his kiss as hot, as sexy, as overwhelming as she remembered from the previous night. She hadn't been embellishing the details.

His arms held her close to his yummy body, his need as apparent to her as the need pulsing along her veins.

When he lifted his mouth away she put her hands up and brought his head back to hers. She liked him kissing her. More than any man before. *Scary. Don't think about what that means right now. Don't think at all. Enjoy the moment.* Her tongue slipped across his bottom lip, tasting him, sending enough heat to her legs to make them momentarily incapable of holding her upright without holding on to Flynn tighter.

'Ally, you're doing it to me again. Sending me over the edge so quickly I can't keep up.' Thankfully he returned to kissing as soon as he stopped talking.

So not the moment for talking. This was when mouths had other, better, things to do. Since when had kissing got to be so wonderful anyway? Or was it just Flynn's kisses that turned her on so rapidly? Before Flynn she'd thought they were just a prelude to bedroom gymnastics, but now she could honestly spend the whole evening just kissing.

Then his hands slid under her top to touch her skin and she knew she'd been fooling herself. She had to have him, skin to skin, hips to hips. Hands touching, teasing, caressing. Now. Pulling her mouth free, she growled, 'The couch or your bedroom?'

His eyes widened, then he shook his head. 'Bedroom. There's a lock on the door.'

She hadn't had to think about children barging in before. But why did Flynn have a lock on his bedroom door? Did he do this often? No, he'd told her she was the first since Anna died. Somehow she knew he hadn't lied to her. Whatever the reason it was there, she was grateful or Flynn wouldn't have continued with this even with Adam sound asleep.

He said, 'I'm hoping you've got more of those condoms in your bag.'

'That's what the pharmacy's handy for. Called in at the one farthest from the clinic on my way back from visiting a patient.' No point in creating gossip if she didn't have to.

Flynn laughed. 'You don't honestly think they won't know who you are already?'

Her fingers caught his chin and pulled that talkative mouth down for another kiss. 'Let's get back to where we were.'

'Now who's talking too much?'

They both shut up from then on, too busy touching and stroking, kissing, undressing one another as their desire coiled tighter and tighter. And tighter.

The phone woke Ally. It was a local number, though not one she knew. Seven o'clock on a Saturday morning. She might not know many people on this island, but it seemed someone always wanted to get her out of bed before she was ready. Or in bed, as with Flynn.

'Ally, is that you? It's Chrissie.'

'Hey, Chrissie, what's up?" Ally pushed up the bed to lean back against her pillow.

'I'm bleeding. I'm not losing the baby, am I?' Her voice rose.

'First of all, take a deep breath and try to calm down. I'll have to examine you to know the answer to that, but you're not necessarily having a miscarriage. Sometimes women do have some spotting and it's fine.'

'But what if I am miscarrying?' There were tears in Chrissie's voice. 'I don't want to lose it.'

Ally felt her heart squeeze for this brave young woman. 'How heavy is the bleeding?' Wrong question. To every pregnant mother it would be a flood.

'Not lots. Nothing like my period or anything.'

Got that wrong, then, didn't I? 'I'll come and see you this morning. Try to relax until I get there. This could just be due to hormonal changes or an irritation to your cervix after sex.' Had Chrissie been seeing the boy who'd had a part in this pregnancy? There'd still been no mention of the father and she was reluctant to ask. It wasn't any of her business, unless Chrissie was under undue pressure from him about the pregnancy and so far that didn't seem to be the case.

'Really?' Chrissie's indrawn breath was audible on the phone. Girls of this age didn't usually like talking about their sexual relations to the midwife. It was *embarrassing*. 'But that didn't happen before when I wasn't pregnant.'

'Your body is changing all the time now, and especially your cervix.' It sounded like they might have the cause of the spotting, but she needed to make absolutely sure. Ally got up and stretched, her body aware of last night's love-making with Flynn. Easing the kinks out of her neck and back, she used one hand to pull on a thick jersey and trackpants before making her way to the kettle for a revitalising coffee. 'Have you told your mum what's happening?'

'Yes. She said to ring you or Dr Reynolds.'

And I got the vote. Warmth surged through her. 'If I'm at all worried after the exam, you'll still need to see Dr Reynolds. He might want you to have an ultrasound. But first things first. I'll be at your house soon. Is that all right?' She wouldn't mention the blood tests she'd need samples for. Chrissie might've sailed through the last lot without a flinch, but she didn't need to be stressed over today's until the last minute.

'Thank you, Ally. That's cool. I'm sorry to spoil your day off.'

'Hey, you haven't. This is what being a mid-wife's about. You wait until junior is ready to come out. He or she won't care what day of the week it is, or even if it's day or night.'

'I'm going to find out if it's a boy or girl. I want time to think of a name and to get some nice things for it. I feel weird, calling the baby "it". Like I don't care or something.'

Talking about the scan was more positive than worrying she might be losing the baby. Ally sighed with relief. 'Catch you shortly.'

Four hours later Ally parked outside Flynn's house and rubbed her eyes. She was unusually tired. Her head felt weighed down—with what, she had no idea. Maybe the slower pace of the island did this to people. She'd noticed not everyone hurried from place to place, or with whatever they were doing. Certainly not the checkout operator at the supermarket, where she'd just been to stock up on a few essentials. The girl had been too busy talking to her pal she'd previously served to get on with the next load of groceries stacked on her conveyor belt.

Tap-tap on her window. Flynn opened her door. 'Hey, you coming in or going to sit out here for the rest of the day? Adam could run errands for you, bring you a coffee or a sandwich.'

'That sounds tempting.' The heaviness lifted a little and she swung out of the car. 'How's things in your house this morning?'

He ignored her question. 'You look exhausted. All that sexercise catching up with you?' He suddenly appeared genuinely concerned. 'You're not coming down with anything, are you?'

'Relax, I'm good. Just tired. I've spent most of this morning with Matilda Livingstone, trying to calm her down and make her understand that her pregnancy is going well, that she doesn't need to worry about eclampsia at this early stage, if at all.'

'Her mother's been bleating in her ear again, I take it?'

'Unfortunately, yes. Such a different outlook from Angela and Chrissie. I had an hour with Chrissie, as well. She had some mild spotting this morning, but hopefully I've allayed her concerns. We talked a lot about the trimesters and what's ahead for her and the baby. I'm amazed at how much detail she wanted to know.'

'Could be her way of keeping on top of the

overwhelming fact that she's pregnant and still at school and hoping to go to university.'

Ally nodded. 'Yes, well, that plan of becoming a lawyer is on hold for a little while, but I bet she will do her degree. Maybe not in the next couple of years, but some time. There's a fierce determination building up in her that she'll not let baby change her life completely, that she's going to embrace the situation and make the most of everything.'

'That's fine until her friends leave the island to study and she's at home with a crying infant. That's the day she'll need all the strength she can muster.'

Ally shook her head at him. 'She'll love her precious baby so much she'll be fine.'

'Spoken like someone who hasn't had a major disappointment in her life.'

Spoken like a woman who's had more than her fair share of those, and has learned to try and see only the best in life by not involving herself with people so they can't hurt her.

'That's me—Pollyanna's cousin.' It shouldn't hurt that Flynn didn't see more to her than her cheery facade, didn't see how forced that sometimes was, but it did. Even if she cut him some slack because it had barely been a week since they'd met and outside work they'd only had fun times, she felt a twinge of regret.

What would it be like to have someone in her life who truly knew her? Where she'd come from. Why she kept moving from one clinic to the next, one temporary house to another. She'd thought she'd won the lottery with the Bartletts. She had come so close to belonging, had been promised love and everything, even adoption, so when it hadn't eventuated, the pain of being rejected for a cute three-year-old had under-scored what she'd always known. She was unlov-able. Letting people into her heart was foolish, and to have risked it to the Bartletts because they'd made promises of something she'd only ever dreamed of having had been the biggest mistake of her young life. So big she'd never contemplated it again.

Oh, they'd explained as kindly as they could how their own two children, younger than her, hadn't wanted a big sister. Being mindful of their children's needs made Mr and Mrs Bartlett good parents, but they should never have promised her the earth. She'd loved them with such devotion it had taken months to fully understand what had happened. They'd said she was always welcome at their home. Of course, she hadn't visited.

As she locked the car she watched Flynn with her bags of goodies striding up the path to his front door. Why did she feel differently about Flynn? Whatever the answer, it was all the more reason to remain indifferent.

Did his confidence come from having loved and been loved so well that despite his loss he knew who he was and why he was here? He wasn't going to share his life with her or another woman. It was so obvious in the way he looked out for Adam, in the balancing act he already had with his career and his son. She'd been aware right from the get-go that there would be no future for her here.

That's how she liked it, remember?

As Flynn stopped to look back at her she knew an almost overwhelming desire to run up to him and throw herself into his arms. So strong was this feeling that she unlocked the car. She had to drive away, go walk the beach or take a visit to the mainland.

'Ally? You gone to sleep on your feet?' The concern was genuine. 'I think you should see a doctor.' Then he smiled that stomach-tightening smile straight at her. 'This doctor.'

How could she refuse that invitation? There was friendship in that smile. There was mischief, as in sex, in that smile. That was more than enough. That's all she ever wanted.

She locked the car again and headed inside.

Flynn watched Ally with Adam. She didn't appear to be overly tired, more distracted. By what? Was she about to tell him thanks, she'd had a blast, but it was over? Already?

He wasn't ready to hear that news. Not yet. They'd just got started. It had come as a surprise to find he wanted her so much, needed to get to know her intimately. He understood it had to be a short-term affair. Ally would leave at the end of her contract in three weeks—no doubt about that. For that he should be grateful. There wasn't room in his life for anyone else. Adam came first, second, and took anything left over from the demands of the clinic.

Anyway, he doubted whether Ally had room

for him or any man in her life. She was so intent on moving on, only touching down briefly in places chosen for her by her bosses and circumstances, doing her job with absolute dedication and then taking flight again.

'Hey, Adam, what've you been doing this morning?' The woman dominating his thoughts was talking to his boy and scratching Sheba's ears.

'We went to the beach to throw sticks for Sheba. I chucked them in the water. That's why she's all wet.' Mischief lightened that deep shade of blue radiating out of Adam's eyes. *Here we go, another round of giggles coming up.*

'The water must've been freezing.' Ally smiled softly and ruffled his hair, which Adam seemed to like. And that simple show of affection put the kibosh on the giggles as he stepped close to Ally and patted the top of Sheba's head, too.

'Sheba likes swimming.' Adam looked up at Ally, hope in his eyes. 'Are you still coming to see the penguins with us?'

'That's why I'm here. You and I can do the funny walk on the beach, see if they want to be our friends.' She was good with him, no doubt about that.

Which set Flynn to more worrying. That look Adam had given her showed how much his boy already felt comfortable with Ally. Though, to be fair, he was comfortable with just about everybody. But was this a good idea, having Ally drop by for lunch and a drive around the island? His boy didn't need to lose anyone else in his life. It was only recently that he'd got past that debilitating grief after Anna's death. *He must not get close to Ally. He could not.*

'Flynn, you've caught the sleeping-on-your-feet bug.' Ally had crossed to his side and was nudging him none too gently in the ribs with her elbow. 'You with us?'

He relaxed. Let the sudden fire in his belly rule his head. 'You bet. Do you want to come back for dinner tonight?' *Afterwards we could have some more of that bedroom exercise.*

'Did you have anything else in mind for the evening? There's a wicked glint in your baby blues.'

'Dessert maybe.'

'With whipped cream?' Her tongue slid across her lips and sent heat to every corner of his body.

So this was what it was like to wake up after a long hibernation. Not slowly, but full-on wide-awake and ready to go. Making love with this woman had been like a promise come true. Exciting and beautiful. He wanted to do it again and again. *Making love as against having sex? Now, there's something to think about.*

'Can I have ice cream, too?' Adam asked, bringing them back to earth with a thud.

'We can get cones when we're out this afternoon.' How many hours before Adam was tucked up in bed fast asleep? How long until he could kiss Ally until she melted against him?

'Flynn,' she mock growled. 'We have plans for this afternoon. Let's get them under way, starting with lunch. My shout at a café or wherever you recommend near this penguin colony. The busier we are, the quicker the day will go by.'

'Can't argue with that.' She was so right he had to drop a kiss on her cheek as a reward. It would've been too easy to move slightly and cover her mouth with his. Thank goodness common sense prevailed just in time and he stepped back to come up with, 'I'm thinking of getting our flippers out of the cupboard in the garage so that you two human penguins can flip-flop along the beach.'

'Can we, Dad? Ally, want to?' Adam yelled, as he ran in the direction of the garage internal door.

Flynn waved a hand after him. 'Go easy on that cupboard door. You know what happened last time you opened it.'

'I'll help him.' Ally was already moving in the same direction, her fingers tracing the spot on her cheek he'd just kissed.

'Good idea. Things tend to spill all over the place when he starts poking through the junk on the shelves.' He relaxed. Adam was excited, and Ally was just being a part of that, helping make his day more fun. It wasn't like she'd moved in or would see him every day of the week. She'd be gone soon enough, and Adam would still have all his playmates and the many adults on the island who enjoyed spoiling and looking out for him. He'd be safe. He wasn't in danger of getting hurt.

Flynn paused. Neither was he. Despite being

equally excited as his boy. Ally hadn't said anything about calling their affair—if that's what it was—quits yet, so he'd carry on for three more weeks and make the most of her company. It wasn't as though he'd be broken-hearted when she went, mad, crazy attraction for her and all. He'd miss her for sure. She was the woman who'd woken him up, but that didn't mean he had to have her in his life permanently.

CHAPTER SIX

'WHERE'S DAD?' ADAM bounced into the bedroom and jumped up on the bed, effectively ending any pretence of Ally sleeping.

Groaning, she rolled over to stare up at this little guy. Something warm and damp nudged her arm. Turning her head, she came eye to eye with Sheba. Another groan escaped her. So this was what it was like to wake up in a family-orientated house. Kind of cosy, though it would've been better if Flynn were here.

'Why are you here?' Adam asked, looking around as though he might find his father in the wardrobe or on the floor beside the bed.

'Dad had to go to work so I stayed to look after you.'

'Did someone have a crash?' No four-year-old should look so knowledgeable about his father's work.

'Yes, during the night.' The call had come

through requesting Flynn's presence as Ally had been about to walk out the door to return to the flat. They'd agreed she shouldn't be there in the morning with him when Adam woke up. But when the call came Flynn had been quick to accept her offer to stay, so apparently he could break his own rules.

Jerome had picked up Flynn ten minutes later. Teens had been racing on the bridge in the wee hours of the morning after too much alcohol. Two cars had hit side on and spun, slamming into the side of the bridge, injuring four lads. Carnage, Flynn had told her when he'd phoned to explain he wouldn't be back until early morning as he was accompanying one of the boys to the Royal Melbourne Hospital.

'He doesn't like going to crashes. They're yucky.' Adam patted the bed and the next thing Ally felt the bed dipping as Sheba heaved herself up to join them.

'Is she allowed on the bed?' Ally shuffled sideways to avoid being squashed by half a ton of Labrador.

'Sometimes.'

'Right, and today's one of those times. Why

did I not see that coming?' She chucked him under the chin. About to sit up, she stopped. Under the covers she wore only underwear. Definitely not the kind that decently covered all the girl bits. 'Adam, do you think you could take Sheba out to the kitchen while I get up?' Her clothes were in a tangled heap on the floor where she'd dropped them before climbing back into bed after Flynn had left.

'Do you want Dad's dressing gown? It's in the wardrobe. He never uses it.' Adam leapt off the bed, obviously unperturbed that she was there. Maybe he could explain that to his father. 'He walks around with no clothes on when he gets up in the morning.'

Too much information. At least while Flynn wasn't there and this little guy was. But she could picture Flynn buck naked as he strolled out to put the kettle on. Seriously sexy. 'I'd love the dressing gown.'

Adam had just dumped the robe on the bed when they both heard the front door opening. 'Dad's back.' He raced through the house, Sheba lumbering along behind him.

Making the most of the opportunity Ally

slipped out of bed and into the dressing gown, tying the belt tightly around her waist. A glance in the mirror told her that as a fashion statement, an awful lot was lacking. Her face could do with a scrub, too. All that mascara had worked its way off her lashes and smudged her upper cheeks.

In the kitchen she plugged in the coffee maker and leaned her hip against the bench, waiting for the males of this house to join her.

Flynn sloped into the kitchen, with Adam hanging off his back like a monkey. Sheba brought up the rear. 'Morning, Ally. Sleep well?'

Huh?

Then he winked and she grinned. 'Like a lizard.'

'Like your outfit,' he tossed her way.

'I'm not sure about the colour. Brown has never been my favourite shade of anything. Want a coffee?'

'I'd kill for one, but can you give me five? I want to leap under a very hot shower.' His face dropped and his eyes saddened. 'It was messy out there,' he said quietly.

She nodded, wanting to ask more but reluctant to do so in front of Adam. Instead, she reached

a hand to his cheek, cupped his face. 'Go and
scrub up. I'll have the coffee waiting.' *Cosy,
cosy.*

'Ta. You're a treasure.' For a moment she
thought he was going to kiss her. His eyes locked
on hers and he leaned closer. Then he must've
remembered Adam on his back because he
pulled away. 'I won't take long.'

He returned in jeans and a polo-neck black
jersey that showed off his physique to perfection. His feet were bare, his hair a damp mess.
He couldn't have looked more sexy if he'd tried.
It came naturally.

Passing over a mug of strong coffee, she picked
up the container she'd found in the pantry. 'Feel
like croissants for breakfast?'

'Croissants it is. I'll heat them while you have
a shower if you like.' He didn't like her loung-
ing around in his dressing gown? Then his eyes
widened and she realised he was staring at her
cleavage. An exposed cleavage.

Grabbing the edges of the robe, she tugged
them closed. 'As soon as I've finished my coffee I'll get cleaned up.' Then what? Did she head
home after breakfast? It would be fun to hang

out with these two for a while. Talk about getting used to this cosy stuff all too quickly. Today
she was simply ignoring the lessons learned and
taking a chance. At what?

'We always go for a walk on the beach after
breakfast in the weekends. You coming?' Flynn
asked.

'Love to. Were you having a late breakfast
when Sheba bowled me over last Sunday?' she
asked around a smile, suddenly feeling good
about herself. A chance at some normal, everyday fun that families all over the country would
be doing. She wouldn't think about how often
she'd stared through the proverbial window,
longing for exactly this. She wouldn't contemplate next Sunday or the one three weeks away
when she was back in Melbourne. Instead, she'd
enjoy the day and keep the brakes on her emotions.

'No, two walks in one day. Makes up for the
weekdays when she gets short-changed. I don't
like dragging Adam out of bed too early. Marie
walks her occasionally, but I think she's worried
about being knocked over in her pregnant state.'

'Have you known Marie long?'

He nodded. 'Anna and Marie were school friends. They went their separate ways but kept in touch and Anna always talked about when they'd both be living back here with their families.' That sadness was back, this time for himself and his family.

Great. It was hard to compete with a woman who held all the aces and wasn't around any more to make mistakes. *You're competing now? What happened to your fixed-in-concrete motto—Have Fun and Move On?* That was exactly what she was doing. Having fun. And…in three weeks she'd be moving on. So none of this mattered. *Really?* Really. She tried for a neutral tone even when she felt completely mixed up. 'Marie must miss her, too.'

'She does, especially now her first baby's due.'

'What would Marie have to say if she knew about us?' Would she stick up for Anna or accept that Flynn was entitled to get on with his life? *Hello? What does any of that matter? You're out of here soon enough.*

'I have no idea.' Flynn looked taken aback. 'It's nothing to do with her.' But now that Ally had put the question out there he seemed busy trying to figure out the answer.

Am I trying to wreck this fling early? Because Flynn is sure to pull the plug now.

Placing her empty mug in the sink, she headed for the bathroom. The hot water could ease the kinks in her body, but it was unlikely to quieten the unease weaving through her enjoyment of being with Flynn. It was ingrained in her to protect her heart, but already she understood this wasn't a fling she'd walk away from as easily as any other. What worried her was not understanding why. She already knew she was going to miss Flynn.

But she would go. That was non-negotiable.

Sheba and Adam raced ahead of them, one barking and one shouting as they kicked up sand and left huge footprints. Flynn stifled a yawn and muttered, 'Where do they get their energy?'

'Perhaps you should try dry dog pellets for breakfast instead of hot, butter-soaked croissants,' a certain cheeky midwife answered from beside him.

'You're telling me Adam didn't eat a croissant with a banana and half a bottle of maple syrup poured on top? That was all for show and he actually scoffed down dog food?' Breakfast hadn't stacked up against Anna's ideas of healthy eating, but sometimes his boy was allowed to break the rules. Or *he* broke the rules and Adam enjoyed the result.

Ally's shoulder bumped his upper arm as she slewed sideways to avoid stepping on a fish carcass that had washed up on the tide. 'Yuk. That stinks.'

His hand found hers, their fingers interlaced, and he swung their arms between them. For a moment everything bothering him simply disappeared in this simple gesture. How much more relaxed could life get? He and Ally walking along the beach, hand in hand, watching Adam and the dog playing. Right now this was all he needed from life.

Then his phone broke the magic. 'Hello? Flynn Reynolds speaking.'

'This is William Foster's sister, Maisey. He's having chest pains again and refusing to go in the ambulance I called. Can you talk some sense into that stubborn head of his?'

'On my way. Can you hold on a moment?' He didn't wait for her reply. 'Ally, I've got to see a patient urgently. Can you take Adam home for me when you've finished your walk?' Asking for help twice in less than twenty-four hours didn't look like he managed very well. She'd probably be running away fast.

'No problem. Key to the house?'

'I'll need it to get my car out so I'll leave it in the letterbox.' He waved Adam over. 'I've got to see a patient. Ally's going to stay with you, okay?'

'Can we get an ice cream, Ally?' Hope lightened his face.

'No, you can't.' He wiped that expectancy away. 'Not after that enormous breakfast.' Bending down, he dropped a quick kiss on Adam's forehead. 'See you in a bit, mate.'

'You haven't said goodbye to Sheba.'

'I'm sure she won't mind.' Straightening up, Flynn looked at Ally, leaned in and kissed her cheek. 'Thanks, I owe you.'

Then he started to jog the way they'd come and got back to talking to Maisey. 'I didn't know William had been discharged.'

'He wasn't.'

So the old boy had taken it in his own hands to get out of hospital. 'He definitely needs that talking to, but I have to say I've already tried on more than one occasion and he's never been very receptive to anything I've said.'

'He's lost the will to live.'

That was it in a nutshell. 'I'll talk to his daughter again.' Not that he held out any hope. She'd had no more luck than anyone else.

Glancing over his shoulder, he saw Adam throwing a stick for Sheba, laughing and shouting like only four-year-olds could. *When he's older, will he fight for me if the need arose? I hope I am such a good parent that he will.* Ally drifted into his vision as she chased another stick Adam had thrown, and he felt a frisson of longing touch him. Longing that followed him up and across the road and all the way home.

Longing that wasn't only sexual; longing that reminded him of lazy days with Anna and Adam, of friendship and love. Longing he had no right to explore. He'd been married to the love of his life. No one got a second whack at that. Anyway, as Anna had told him on the day she'd died, he hadn't been the perfect husband. He'd worked too many hours, putting his career before his family apparently. It hadn't mattered that the career had given them the lifestyle they'd had. Yeah, the one Anna apparently hadn't wanted. Not in the middle of Melbourne anyway. *Damn it, Anna, I'm so sorry we were always arguing. I'm sorry about so many things.*

He needed to scrub that from his mind and concentrate. William needed him urgently. Hitting the gas accelerator, he drove as fast as the law allowed—actually, a little faster.

Sure enough, the ambulance was parked in William's driveway. Maisey led him inside, where the paramedics had the heart monitor attached to William's chest. The reading they passed him was abnormal. He inclined his head towards the door, indicating everyone should leave him with his patient for a few minutes.

'Don't even start, Doc,' William wheezed the moment they were alone.

'You think you have the right to decide when you should clock out, do you?'

William blinked. 'It's my life.'

'From the moment you're born, it's not just

yours. You have family, friends, colleagues. They all have a part of you, whether you care or not. Whether you love them or not.'

'I've lost interest in everything since Edna died. You know how it is, Doc.'

Yes, he sure did, but, 'Don't play that card with me, William. Look me in the eye and tell me Edna would want you ignoring your daughter's love? What about your grandchildren, for goodness' sake? What sort of example are you setting them with this attitude? You think teaching them to give up when the going gets tough is good for them?' Flynn sat down and waited. He wouldn't belabour the points he'd made. There was such a thing as overdoing it.

Silence fell between them. The house creaked as the sun warmed it. Somewhere inside he heard Maisey and the paramedics talking. He continued to wait.

William crossed his legs, uncrossed them. His hands smoothed his trousers. He stared around the room, his gaze stopping on a photograph of his family taken when Edna had still been alive.

Flynn held his breath.

William's gaze shifted, focused on a painting of a farmhouse somewhere on the mainland, then moved on to another of a rural scene. Paintings Edna had done.

Flynn breathed long and slow, hoping like hell his patient didn't have another cardiac incident in the next few minutes. What if he'd done the wrong thing? But he'd tried the soft approach. It was time to be blunt. They had to get William aboard that ambulance and manhandling him when he refused to go wasn't the answer—or legal. He had every right to say no. But he'd better not arrest, at least not until he was in hospital.

William had returned to that family photo, his gaze softening, his shoulders dropping a little from their indignant stance. Then one tear slipped from his right eye and slowly rolled down his cheek. He nodded once. 'I'll go. For my Edna.'

Good for you. 'I'll tell the paramedics.' And Maisey, who'd no doubt be phoning her niece the moment William had been driven away.

After Flynn had filled in some paperwork to go with his patient, he talked briefly to Maisey and then headed for his car. He was going home to Adam and Ally. They'd go for a jaunt round to San Remo. If only he didn't feel so drained of energy. Already tired after last night's emergency call-out, talking with William had taken more out of him than he'd have expected. He understood all too well how the other man felt; he also knew William was wrong. Hopefully, one day the old guy would acknowledge that, at least to himself if no one else.

The sunny winter's day had brought everyone out to San Remo to stroll along the wharves and look at the fishing boats tied up. The restaurants and bars were humming as the locals made the most of fewer tourists.

'What's your preference for lunch?' Flynn asked Ally, after they'd walked the length of the township's main street and had bumped into almost the entire register of his patients at the clinic.

'Fish and chips on the beach.' Then she smiled at him.

Her smiles had been slow in coming since he'd returned home, making him wonder if she felt he'd been using her. Which, he supposed, he had, but not as a planned thing. She'd been there when he'd got both calls and he hadn't hesitated to ask her. She could've said no. 'Good answer. There's a rug in the boot of my car we can spread on the sand.'

Had he used Ally by putting his work before what she might've wanted? *Just like old times.* But asking Ally to stay was putting Adam first, just not her. Turning, he touched a finger to her lips. 'Thank you.'

'What for?'

'Being you. I'm going to get lunch.'

'Adam and I will be over on that monster slide.'

'He's conned you into going down that?' Flynn grinned. 'Don't get stuck in the tube section.'

Yep, this felt like a regular family outing. Dad ordering the food, Adam wanting to play with Mum. Except Ally wasn't Mum, and never would be.

Which part of having a short affair had he forgotten? As much as Ally turned him on with the briefest of looks or lightest of touches, no matter how often they fell into bed together, this was only an affair with a limited number of days to run. When was that going to sink in?

While he waited for his order he watched

the woman causing him sleepless nights. She smiled sweetly at his son bouncing alongside her, said something that made him giggle. Then she rubbed her hand over his head, as she often did. How come Adam didn't duck out the way as he did with other people who went to touch him?

Flynn sighed. Should he be getting worried here? How would his boy react when Ally left them? Yes, he'd asked himself this already, and would probably keep doing so until he knew what to do about it. He'd have the answer on the day Ally left.

The real problem was that he didn't want to stop what he and Ally had going on. It was for such a short time, couldn't he make the most of it? Wasn't he entitled to some fun? If only that's all it was, and the fun didn't come with these conflicting emotions.

The fish and chips were the best he'd ever had, the batter crisp, the fish so fresh it could've still been flapping. The company was perfect.

Ally rolled her eyes as her teeth bit into a piece of fish. 'This is awesome. I'm going to have to starve all week to make up for it.'

As if she needed to watch her perfect figure. 'We'll eat salads every day till next Sunday.'

Surprise widened those beautiful eyes. 'Something you haven't talked to me about yet?'

It had only occurred to him at that moment. 'You might as well join us for dinner every night. I like cooking while you obviously have an aversion to it. Next Saturday we can visit the wildlife centre.' Once he got started, his plan just grew and grew. 'Fancy a return visit to Giuseppe's on Saturday night? It's band night.'

'Don't tell me. The old two-step brigade.' She grinned to take the sting out of her words.

'Way better than that. The college has a rock band that's soon going to compete in a talent show. Giuseppe's way of supporting them is to hire them on Saturday nights. He says the music is crazy.'

'We can crazy dance, then. Yes to all those invitations. Thank you. You've saved me having to stock up on instant meals.' She wrapped up the paper their meal had come in and stood to take it across to a rubbish bin.

'Can we go to the wildlife park now, Dad?'

'Not today, Adam. You've already had a busy weekend, going places that you don't usually visit.'

'But, Dad, why can't I go? Now?'

'Don't push it, son. We're going home. I've got things to do around the house.' Flynn could feel that tiredness settling over him again, stronger this time. He yawned just as Ally sat down on the sand again.

'Can't hack the pace, eh, old boy?'

'I don't know anyone who can run a marathon first up after no practice for years.' Not that making out with Ally felt as difficult as running a marathon. It all came too naturally.

'So that's why we do sprints.' Her grin turned wicked and the glint in her eyes arrowed him right in his solar plexus.

It also tightened his groin and reminded him of the intensity of her attraction. They'd be waiting hours before they could act on the heat firing up between them. Adam did put a dampener on the desire running amok in his veins.

'Dad, we're going to the school tomorrow.'

'What school? What are you talking about?' First he'd heard of it.

'Where the big kids go. Marie's taking me with the play group to see what it's like.'

He'd phone Marie when they got home. 'Are you sure?' This sounded like something he should be doing. 'That's my job, taking you there. I'm your parent, not Marie.'

Ally put a hand on his forearm. 'Wait till you've talked to her. Adam might've got it wrong.' The voice of reason was irritating.

'I doubt it. Marie should've mentioned it. She knows that when it comes to the major parenting roles I'll do them. Not her or anyone else.' Now he sounded peevish, but he *was* peeved. 'I'm doing what Anna would've wanted. What I want. I'm not a surface parent, supplying warmth and shelter and avoiding everything else going on in Adam's life. No, thank you.'

She pulled her hand away, shoved it under her thigh. 'Has anyone suggested otherwise?' An edge had crept into her tone.

Had he come across too sharply? Probably. 'Sorry, but you don't understand.' Had she just ground her teeth? 'When Anna was alive she did most things with Adam. We agreed she'd be a stay-at-home mother, and when she died I wanted nothing more than to stay at home with him, but of course that's impossible.'

'How can you say I don't understand? What do you know about me? I might have ten kids back in Melbourne.'

'Perhaps you should try telling me something.' He drew a calming breath. This was crazy, arguing because Adam might be going to school with Marie tomorrow. It wasn't Ally's fault he hadn't known or that he felt left out. 'Have you had a child?' he asked softly after a few minutes. Had she been a teenage mother who'd had her baby adopted?

'No,' she muttered, then again, a lot louder. 'No. Never.'

'Got younger brothers and sisters, then?'

Now her hands fisted on her thighs. 'No.'

He backed off a bit, changed direction with his quest for knowledge about her. 'Why did you choose midwifery as your specialty?' Was that neutral enough? Or was her reason for becoming a midwife something to do with her past? A baby she wasn't admitting to?

'I wanted to be a midwife after helping deliver my foster-mother's baby at home when I was fifteen. The whole birthing process touched something in me. I'd never seen a newborn before and I knew immediately I wanted to be a part of the process.'

Flynn wanted to know how Ally had found herself in that situation, but he didn't dare ask. Instead, he said, 'Birth is pretty awe-inspiring.'

'You're saying that from a parent's perspective.' She stared out beyond the beach at who knew what. 'My foster-mother let me hold the baby and when she asked for him back I struggled to let him go. He was beautiful and perfect and tiny. And vulnerable.'

Flynn sat quietly, afraid to say anything in case she closed down.

'For the first time in my life I'd experienced something so amazing that I wanted to do it again and again.' Her fingers trailed through the sand. 'I felt a connection—something I'd never known in my life.'

The eyes that finally locked onto his knocked the air out of his lungs. The pain and loneliness had him reaching for her, but she put a hand on his chest to stay him, saying, 'Until that moment I'd supposed birth and babies were things to be avoided at all cost. My own mother abandoned me when I was only days old.'

He swore. Short and sharp but full of anger for an unknown woman. How could anyone do that? How could Ally's mother not have wanted her? But, then again, as a doctor he'd seen plenty of people who just couldn't cope. Drug problems, mental illness, abusive partners—sometimes bringing up a baby was beyond people when they couldn't even take care of themselves.

She continued as though she hadn't uttered such a horrific thing. 'There was something so special about witnessing a new life. New beginnings and hope, that instant love from the mother to her baby.' Ally blinked but didn't cry. No doubt she'd used up more than her share of tears over the years. 'It doesn't matter how many births I've attended, each one rips me up while also giving me hope for the future.'

'Yet you don't stay around long enough to get involved with your mums and their babies.'

'No.'

So Ally didn't believe in a happy future for herself.

Her laugh was brittle as she shifted the direction of the conversation. 'I had one goal—to become a midwife. Shortly after my foster-mother's baby arrived, I went back into a group home, but I enrolled for night lessons at high school and worked my backside off during the day. Finally I made it to nursing school and then did the midwifery course and here I am.' The words spilled out as though she wanted this finished. But she couldn't hide her pride.

'It must've been darned hard work.' Lots of questions popped into his head, questions he doubted she'd answer. Ally looked exhausted after revealing that much about herself. It obviously wasn't something she did often—or at all.

The drive home was quiet. Flynn's forefingers drummed a rhythm on the steering wheel as his frustration grew. He'd learnt something very important about Ally that had briefly touched on who she was, and yet it wasn't enough. There had to be so much behind what he'd heard, things she obviously kept locked up, and he needed to hear them. How else could he help her?

'Dad, stop. You're going past our house.'

Flynn braked, looked around. 'Just checking to see if you were awake.'

Ally stared at him like he'd grown another nose. 'It's dangerous not to concentrate when you're driving.'

Because she was right and he didn't want to tell her what had distracted him, he ignored her and pressed the automatic garage door opener.

Inside the house, Flynn reached for the kettle. 'What would you like to do now, Ally?'

She tensed briefly then shook her head. 'You know what? I'm going to head back to the flat. I've got a few chores that need doing.'

His heart lurched. 'Thank you for sharing some of your story.'

Her deliberate shrug closed him off from her. 'I'm just your regular girl. And this regular girl needs to do some washing and answer some emails before work tomorrow.'

He wanted to insist she stay and share a light dinner, watch a movie on TV with him, but for once he knew when to shut up. 'Okay. I'll see you in the morning, then.'

CHAPTER SEVEN

ALLY DROPPED HER keys on the bench and stared around Kat's flat. Not grand on any scale, but a cosy and comfortable bolthole for Kat at the end of her day, a place to kick off her shoes and be herself. A place to face the world from.

What had possessed her to spill her guts to Flynn? At least he'd understand why she wasn't mother material. But it was Adam's laughing face cruising through her mind, teasing her with hope when in reality she wasn't ready for a child, would never be. Ally caressed her two ornamental dogs, her mouth twisted in sadness. Real-life pets required stability in their lives. The idea of owning a home hadn't made it onto her list of goals for the next ten years. She faced everything the world threw her way by digging deep and putting on a mask. She didn't need bricks and mortar to hide behind. Honestly, she had no idea about setting up a home that she could feel comfortable in.

Would I feel more content, less alone, if I had a place I could call home? A place—the same place—to live in between jobs, instead of bunking with whoever has a spare bed?

Sweat broke out on her upper lip. Her stomach rolled with a sickening sensation. Thirty-one and she'd never had a home, not even as a child. Those foster-homes she'd lived in had been about survival, not about getting settled. She'd always tried so hard to please her foster-parents in the desperate hope they'd fall in love with her and adopt her, but that had never happened. The only time she'd believed she might be there long term had ended in tears and her packing her few possessions to take to the next stop in her life. She'd finally wised up to the fact—starting with her own mother—that no one cared for her enough to give her what she craved.

Don't go there. You've been over and over and over trying to understand why she left you on a stranger's doorstep. There is no answer.

Poking around in her bag, she found her music player, put the earbuds in and turned the volume up loud. Music helped to blot out the memories. Sometimes.

Then her phone vibrated against her hip and broke through her unease. Removing the earbuds, she answered the phone. 'Hey, Lilia, glad you rang.' Curling up on the settee she sighed with relief. A bit of girl talk would send those other thoughts away. 'What have you been up to?'

Lilia had refused to be pushed away while she'd been on a job in Lilia's home town, and they'd become friends despite her wariness.

'Just the usual. What about you? Having a blast on the island?'

'Yep, it's great.'

'Try to sound like you mean that,' Lilia said. 'Not like you've been sent to the middle of nowhere with no man in sight.'

That might've been boring, but it would've been safer. Flynn was sneaking in under her radar. She drew a breath and found some enthusiasm. 'Oh, there are men here. Even downright drop-dead sexy ones.'

'Ones, as in many? Or one? As in you're having fun?'

'One. Dr Flynn Reynolds. Do you know him? He used to work at one of Melbourne's hospitals, left about two years ago.'

'The name doesn't ring any bells, and I can't picture him. Is he a GP?'

'A GP, a widower and father of one. Perfect for a short fling.'

'Why do I hear a note of uncertainty?' Lilia suddenly laughed. 'Oh, my God, don't tell me you've gone and fallen for him? You? Miss Staying Single For Absolutely Ever? I don't believe it.'

'That's good because it's not true.' Not true. Not true. Her heart thudded so loudly Lilia probably heard it. Her fingers gripped the phone. 'We've been doing the leg-over thing, even taken the dog and kid for a walk, but that's as far as it's going.'

'Taken the kid and dog for a walk?' Lilia shrieked. 'That's Domesticity 101. You are *so* toasted.'

Panic began clawing through Ally, chilling her, cranking her heart rate up. 'Seriously.' She breathed deeply. 'Seriously, it's all about the sex. Nothing else.'

Lilia was still laughing. 'Go on, tell me some more. Is this Flynn gorgeous?'

'Yes, damn it, he is.'

'Good. Is he a great dad?'

'What's that got to do with anything?' The panic elbowed her. Adam was happy, but even if he wasn't, that had nothing to do with her. Unless she was contemplating having babies with the man. The phone hit the floor with a crash.

Slowly bending to retrieve the phone, she couldn't think of what to say to Lilia. She didn't know what to think, full stop.

Fortunately, Lilia had no such difficulty. 'What happened? You okay? I'm sorry if I've upset you. You know I mean nothing when I say these things.'

Swallow. 'Sure. I dropped the phone, that's all.' Another swallow. 'Lilia, what if I did like Flynn? I can't do anything about it. I know nothing about families or looking after kids or playing house.'

'Hey, girlfriend, go easy on yourself. You're so much better than you think. You're capable of anything you set your mind to. I know you

haven't told me everything, but how you handled putting yourself through school and getting a degree shows that in bucketloads. Do you
really like him?'

Unfortunately, it could be shaping up that way.
It would explain her unease and sudden need
to re-evaluate her life. But it was early days.
She'd soon be out of here and so would whatever
feelings she was dealing with. She'd settle back
to her normal, solo life and forget Flynn. Easy.
'He's okay. So how's it going in Turraburra? Any
interesting men coming your way?'

'That's why I rang.' Lilia got a giant-sized hint
without having to be bashed over the head. 'You
know Noah Jackson, don't you?'

'Enough to say hello to and swap a sentence or
two about our weekends whenever I bump into
him, which isn't often as I rarely see the surgical
teams. Seems an okay guy, though.' She turned
the tables. 'You interested in him?'

'I've heard he's starting here in a month or so,
apparently.'

'He can't be. You've got the wrong guy. Noah
doesn't do general practice. He's a senior surgical registrar, not a GP. Great guy he may be,

but he's very determined to get to the top of his career—and that does not include sitting and talking to mothers and their colicky babies in a small town.'

Lilia sniffed. 'Nothing wrong with general practice.'

'I know that. But I can't see Noah fitting into it. Nah, you've got the wrong guy. The Noah I know wouldn't be seen dead in a place like Turraburra.'

'Well, I heard he'll be with us for four weeks. Perhaps it's a mistake.'

'Well, if he does turn up, the good news is he's a seriously good-looking dude and definitely sexy.' Didn't set her hormones dancing but plenty of women drooled over him.

No, her hormones got a kick out of a certain doctor living here on the island. She had to get a grip, put any stupid concerns behind her and get the job done. Three weeks to go. Twenty-one days. Couldn't be too hard to have some fun and not get involved with the source of that fun. Face it, Flynn no more wanted or needed anything more connected than she did. He definitely wouldn't want Adam getting too attached to her, and she felt exactly the same. More than anything, she couldn't abide hurting that cute wee boy because she understood more than most what it was like to be left behind or shunted on. And she certainly would never be moving into their home and becoming super-mum.

'You still with me?' Lilia interrupted her musings.

'All ears. When are you coming down to Melbourne next?'

After Lilia hung up, Ally went to tug on her running shoes and shorts. A good hard pounding of the pavement would help what ailed her and put everything back into perspective.

'You've got a busy morning stacked up,' Flynn greeted her the moment she walked into the medical centre the next morning. 'Seems word's out that we've got a great new midwife and everyone who's pregnant wants to meet you.' His smile was friendly, but there was caution in his eyes. Did he think she might start considering staying on?

Returning his smile, she shrugged. 'I won't

be delivering most of them. Kat will be back before long.'

His smile dipped. 'The islanders are friendly, that's all it's about. Bet you get an invitation or two for a meal before the morning's out.'

'Cool. But I'm all booked up—most nights anyway.' She locked eyes with Flynn. He hadn't changed his mind on her joining him and Adam for dinners, had he? Of course, she should be backing off a little, but how when right this moment her body was bending in his direction in anticipation of being woken up again? *Back off.* Easy to say, hard to do.

'So you'll come to dinner tonight. I'm glad.' At last the caution disappeared. His smile widened, brought a different kind of warmth to her.

A warmth that touched her deep inside in that place she went when alone. A warmth she hadn't realised she'd needed until she'd walked in and seen him. She'd missed him overnight. Had reached out to hug him and come up empty-handed—empty-hearted as well. 'Babies withstanding, I'll be there at six. Is that okay?'

He leaned close, whispered, 'Bring your toothbrush.'

That warmth turned to heat, firing colour into her chilled cheeks and tightening her stomach. 'Think I'll buy a spare,' she whispered back, before entering the office to collect the notes in her tray.

Megan winked at her. 'Have a good weekend?'

How much had she heard? Ally bit back a retort. She and Flynn would have to learn to be far more careful. 'I went to San Remo.'

Megan laughed. 'Was that you I saw out running late yesterday?'

'Running?' Flynn looked surprised.

'As in putting one foot in front of the other at a fast pace.'

'That explains...' He spluttered to a stop as Megan's eyes widened. 'A lot,' he added lamely. 'Come on, meeting time.'

As she led the way to the staffroom, she wanted to turn around and wrap her arms around him. She wanted to feel his body against hers, his chest against her cheek, his shoulder muscles under her palms. She kept walking, facing directly ahead. She wouldn't be distracted by Flynn at work. She wouldn't. It was all very well for the others to know they'd had a meal out together, might even be aware they'd spent hours doing things over the weekend, but she couldn't show how her body craved his.

'Meeting's cancelled.' Faye barrelled out of her office. 'Flynn, we're needed at the school. Two kids on bikes have been hit by a car. Where's Toby?'

'Do you need me to come along?' Ally asked.

'No, we're sorted.' Faye sped to the back door and the car park, her medical bag in one hand.

Flynn glanced around, quickly dropped a kiss on Ally's mouth. 'See you later.' And he was gone.

Leaving her with her finger pressing her lips, holding that kiss in place. Yeah, she really had missed him all night. But she'd be seeing him tonight. The knot in her tummy loosened as she headed to her room and prepared for her first mum of the day.

Her relaxed mood stayed in place all day, and when she knocked on Flynn's door that night, she didn't hold back on her smiles.

'Ally, you came,' Adam swung the door wide, inadvertently letting Sheba out.

'Sheba, no,' Ally made a grab for her collar. 'Inside, you big lump.'

Sheba replied with a tongue swipe on her hand.

'Now the woman insults my dog.' Flynn stood behind Adam, grinning at her.

Were they both as happy to see her as she was them? Stepping inside, she closed the door behind her, shutting off the world and entering the cosy cocoon that was the Reynolds home. 'Sheba knows I think she's awesome.' Then she had a brainwave. 'I could take her with me when I go running.'

Flynn's eyebrows rose. 'She'd probably have a heart attack. Walks are one thing, but a run?'

'I'm not very quick. More of a snail.' She followed Flynn and Adam into the kitchen, suddenly very aware that by making that suggestion she'd committed herself to this little family for the rest of her stay. As she had that morning when she'd said she would be here for dinners. Nothing wrong with that, as long as she kept everything in perspective. As long as Adam didn't get too close and miss her when she left.

Flynn said, 'See how you go. You might find

you just want to get on the beat and not have to swing by to collect her.'

Was he having second thoughts, too?

'Can I run, too?' Adam asked hopefully.

'No,' Flynn said emphatically.

As his little face began to crumple, Ally explained. 'It's usually very early when I go.'

'It's not fair.'

'Adam, you can't do everything just because you want to. Ally's told you why you can't go with her so leave it at that.' Worry filtered into Flynn's eyes as he watched his son stomp away. When Adam turned on the TV, Flynn growled. 'Turn it off, please.'

Ally glanced from Flynn to his boy's sulky face. 'Has he been naughty?'

'He's not allowed to watch TV often. Anna was against it.'

Ah, Anna's rules. 'Surely a little time watching kids' programmes can't hurt?' *Mind your own business.* 'Other kids don't turn out as delinquents because of it.' *Shut up.*

Flynn stared at Adam, not her. 'It's hard to let go. You know?'

No, she didn't. 'Fair enough. But Adam needs to fit in with his peers at times.'

'You have a point, I guess.' Then he changed the subject. 'How was your day? Angela called me, full of praise for the way you've handled Chrissie's crisis. She doesn't want you leaving before the baby's born.'

Sliding onto a stool and propping her elbows on the bench, she shook her head. 'Chrissie will be fine with Kat.'

Flynn nodded. 'Sure she will. It's just that with Chrissie being so young and this not being a planned pregnancy, she's taken a shine to you and won't be keen to start over. But it'll work out.'

'It has to.'

'It does, doesn't it?'

Ally stared at him. What did that mean exactly? 'I was never going to be here any longer than the month Kat's away.'

He locked his eyes with hers. 'I know. But sometimes I find myself wishing you were.'

Pow. That hit right in the solar plexus, and knocked her heart. Never in a million years would she have thought he'd say something like that. 'A month's long enough for a fling. Any longer and we'd have to start wondering just what we were doing.'

'You ever had a long-term relationship?' He picked up a wooden spoon and stirred the gravy so hard a glob flicked out onto the stovetop.

'No.' She reached for a cloth to wipe up the gravy.

'Never?'

'Never. I go for short flings. Makes leaving the job easier.' *Don't ask me any more.*

'Surely you haven't always moved around as much as you currently seem to do?' He'd stopped stirring, instead studying her as though she was an alien.

Compared to him and his normal family life, she probably was different to the point of being weird. 'I spent two years in Sydney while I went to school, then moved to Melbourne for the years it took to get my degree.' Which had seemed like for ever at the time. She wouldn't mention how often she'd moved flats during those years.

Reaching across to put her hand on his, she pushed the spoon around the pot. 'You're burning the gravy.' His hand was warm under hers, and she squeezed it gently. This was so intimate—in a way she'd never known before—that tears threatened. Tugging her hand away, she stood up and went to set the table.

Flynn watched Ally banging down cutlery on the table. She was hiding something. The answer hit him hard. *More of her past.* What was so bad that she couldn't talk about it? He wouldn't judge her, but maybe he could help her. From what little she'd disclosed about being abandoned, he'd surmised that she'd grown up in the welfare system. Had she gone off the rails as a teen? Asking her outright wouldn't get him any answers, more likely her usual blunt response of no or yes. Those tight shoulders showed the chance of learning anything tonight was less than winning the lottery and he never bought tickets.

He'd told her about Anna. *You call all of about five sentences spilling your guts?* He hadn't said he and Anna had been in love from the first day they'd met at university or all the promises he'd made about Adam at her funeral.

'When's dinner? I'm hungry.'

'Now, there's a surprise.' He saw Ally wink

at his son and then Adam started showing off to her.

Yeah, Adam definitely liked her a lot. So did he. Enough to want more than this affair she was adamant was going nowhere? He began dishing up, thinking how he'd never once considered he might feel something for another woman. Anna had been his everything. Hard to believe he might want a second chance at love.

The pot banged onto the stove top. Love? Get outta here. No way. Too soon, too involved, too impossible.

'You all right?' Ally stood in front of him, studying him carefully.

Swallowing hard, he nodded. 'Of course. Here…' He handed her a plate and was shocked to see his hand shaking.

'You sure?' Her gaze had dropped to his hand. 'Flynn?'

'It's nothing,' he growled. 'Adam, sit up.'

Ally did that irritating shrug of hers and picked up Adam's plate just as he reached for it. Rather than play tug of war, Flynn backed off and headed for his seat at the table. As he gulped his water he struggled to calm down. It wasn't Ally's fault he'd just had a brain melt. But love? Not likely. He needed some space to think about this. How soon could he ask her to go home for the night? Guess she'd want to eat dinner first, though the way she was pushing the food around with her fork she wasn't so keen any more. 'Chicken not your favourite food?'

'I eat more chicken than anything.' She finally took a mouthful, but instead of her eyes lighting up she was thoughtful as she chewed. Swallowing, she asked, 'Do we have a problem? Would you like me to leave?'

Yes. No. 'Not really.' Damn it. 'Sorry. Please stay. For a while at least. I'd like to get to know you better and I can't do that if you're back at Kat's flat.' He'd taken a risk, but he had to learn more about her. Had to.

Her smile was wobbly. 'You want to know more about me? You are hard up for entertainment.'

Another diverting answer, but he wasn't going to be fobbed off any more. He'd start with something innocuous. 'What sort of books do you read?'

'Suspense and thrillers. The darker the better. You?'

'I'm more into autobiographies, especially of people who battle the odds to achieve their goals. Solo round-the-world sailors, mountain climbers, those kinds of people.' Definitely not dark, but it was staggering what a person could achieve if he was determined enough.

Her mouth curved deliciously. 'You're not a suppressed endurance man who wants to battle the odds, are you?'

He shuddered. 'Definitely not. I've got too much respect for my limbs to go off doing something that crazy. Quite happy to read about others' exploits, but that's as far as I go.'

'That's a relief. For a moment there I got worried. Think of that guy who recently tried to kayak from Australia to New Zealand. It must've been incredibly hard for his wife to have to wait for him to make it safe and sound.'

But you're not my partner, so why would you be worried? 'That's why I won't be letting Adam do anything remotely dangerous until he's old and decrepit.'

He leaned back in his chair as the tension eased

out of him. They were back on safe ground and suddenly he didn't want to ask even about the weather in case he put her on edge again. He enjoyed her company too much to chance her leaving early.

'Good luck with that.' She chuckled.

Unfortunately, Ally was referring to Adam. Or so he thought until Ally came around to stand by him, putting a finger on his chin, pressuring him to look at her. She bent to kiss him, softly, sweetly, and still the passion came through fiery and urgent.

At last they'd moved past that earlier little conundrum. The last thing he wanted was to watch Ally walk out the front door tonight. The only place he wanted to be with her was in his bed, making love, tangling the sheets around their legs and holding her so close they'd be as one. He returned her kiss, hard and fierce, trying to convey his need for her.

When she stepped back her eyes were slumberous and that hazel colour had darkened. How soon could he insist Adam go to bed? Because they'd be heading down the hall the moment his son closed his eyes.

Tonight he'd make up for sleeping alone last night. He'd pleasure Ally so much she'd never contemplate a night without him again while she was on the island. Hopefully then this crazy, wonderful desire for her might calm down enough for him to make rational decisions about where they were going with their fling. Ally's word, not his.

Though maybe a fling was still all he needed, and the fact that sex had become alien to him over the last two years could be the answer to why he was reacting like a teenager who'd finally discovered sex.

Ally nudged him in his side. 'Can I read Adam's stories tonight?'

Adam shrieked, 'Yes.'

Flynn spanked her gently on the bottom. 'Anything to get out of doing the dishes.'

She wriggled her butt under his hand. 'Just speeding up the process.'

Of course, Adam had no intention of settling down and going to sleep after only one story. He must've caught the vibes playing between Flynn and Ally because he was wide-awake. 'He's hyper. Unusual for him,' Flynn muttered to Ally when he looked in to see what the delay was.

'It's all right. We're having fun.'

'I'll make coffee, then.' *Go to sleep, Adam. Please, please. Oh, damn it, just go to sleep. I'm going to explode with need any minute.*

He listened as Ally read on, and on, and on. And told himself off for wanting to deny Adam his time with her. Adam came first. First.

Finally, an hour later than he'd hoped, Flynn swung Ally up into his arms and carried her to his bedroom, locking the door behind them. He stood her on her feet and leaned in to kiss that mouth that had been teasing him all night. 'At last.'

Ally already had her shirt over her head, and was pushing those magnificent breasts into his hands. 'You talk too much.'

So he shut up and showed her how much he wanted her, and gave her everything he had.

CHAPTER EIGHT

THE DAYS FLEW by but the nights went even faster. Ally had never known a placement to be so engaging. Was that entirely down to Flynn? Yes, if she was being honest, Flynn owned it— made her dizzy with excitement, warmed her with everyday fun and laughter, distracted her to the point she caught herself wondering how hard it would be to stop in one place for ever.

These heady days hinted at what her childhood dreams had been made of—someone to love her unconditionally for the rest of her life, someone she could give her heart to and not have it returned when the gloss rubbed off. But reality had taught her differently. The only difference now was that she chose where she moved to, and not some overworked, underpaid bleeding heart sitting behind a desk in a dimly lit welfare office. She was no longer a charity case.

Unfortunately, a reality check didn't slow her

enthusiasm for all things Flynn. Her body ached in every muscle, her lips were sore from smiling too much, her eyes were heavy from lack of sleep. But would she wish for quiet nights at Kat's flat with only her music and a book for company? No. Not even knowing that the day of reckoning was approaching made her want to change a thing. The complete opposite, in fact. She found herself needing to grab at more and more time with Flynn.

'Hey,' Flynn called as he walked past the medical storeroom. Then he was in there with her, sucking up all the oxygen and leaving her light-headed. When he traced her chin with his forefinger she caught it and licked the tip, delighting in the sound of his quickly indrawn breath. 'This room's never been so exciting.'

'Are we all set for tonight?' she asked.

'The table's booked at the restaurant. The babysitter's organised. The warning's gone out that no one on Phillip Island is to have an accident.' He ticked the points off his fingers. 'I've put clean sheets on the bed and bought more condoms since we must've used up your supply.'

Her giggle was immature, but that's how she

reacted these days. She was always laughing or coming out with mixed-up, stupid things. 'I go to the supermarket on a regular basis.'

'I was beginning to wonder why you had so many.' He grinned, looking as loony as she felt.

'Everyone on the island must be talking about us by now. In fact, the women are probably giving their men a hard time about how many condoms we're getting through.' She didn't care at all. Every night she raced home to change into something relaxed and less midwife-like, touch up her make-up and put the washing on, then drove around to Flynn's house. She wasn't tired of him at all.

Flynn grinned. 'I'm sure they've all got better things to do than talk about their GP and the midwife.'

'I hope so.' Her heart lurched. That grin always got her behind the knees, making her nearly pitch forward onto her face. For a casual fling Flynn was breaking all the rules and turning her to mush, making her heart skip when no one had done that to her before. 'Does Giuseppe know we're returning to his restaurant?'

'I spoke to him earlier. He's planning a special meal for us. Unless there's something you don't like to eat, we are to sit back and let the courses come.'

'Sounds wonderful.' She planned on wearing a dress tonight, a short black number that she'd found in one of the local shops during her lunch break yesterday. It looked fantastic with her knee-high boots and black patterned stockings. She wouldn't be wearing anything else, bras and knickers being expendable.

'Are you two going to spend the day in that room?' Faye muttered loudly as she stomped past the door. 'There are patients waiting for both of you.'

Guilt had Ally leaping back from Flynn. 'Onto it,' she called out. 'Seriously, Doctor, you should know better than to kiss the nurse at work.'

'I'll do it out in the open next time.' His finger flicked her chin lightly. 'I'll pick you up at seven thirty.'

'I can't wait.' It was true. She'd see him on and off all day and yet she felt desperate to be with him, just the two of them sharing a meal in a restaurant, no interruptions from Adam or the phone or Sheba.

Uh-oh. What was happening? This was starting to feel way wrong. Keep this up and she'd have difficulty leaving at the end of her contract.

'Ally,' Megan called urgently from the office. 'Ally, you're needed. Lisa Shaw's on the line, her waters have broken.'

Now, that was reality. 'Coming.' She picked up her medical bag and dashed to the office, Flynn sent to the back of her mind only to be brought back out when she wasn't helping a baby into the world. This was the real stuff her life was about. The grounded, helping-others kind of thing that gave her the warm fuzzies without asking anything of her heart.

'I'm going to be late.' Ally phoned Flynn at five o'clock when it became obvious Baby Shaw had no intention of hurrying up for anyone, least of all so his mother's midwife could go out to dinner with the local GP. 'I have no idea when Ashton will make his entry. Lisa's contractions slowed nearly two hours ago and so far don't look like speeding up.' Not very medically technical terminology, but he'd get the gist.

'You can't hurry babies.' Disappointment laced

Flynn's words. 'Is it selfish to wish Lisa hadn't wanted a home birth?'

'Yes, it is. I'd better go. I'll call you when I know if we're still on for our date.'

An image of that black dress hanging on the wardrobe door flicked across her mind, and she had to suppress a groan.

Lisa was the only person allowed to groan around here, which she was doing with deep intensity right this moment. Scott held her as she draped her pain-ridden body against him and gritted her teeth.

Ally rubbed Lisa's back. 'You're doing great. Seriously.'

'I have no choice, do I?' Lisa snapped. 'Next time I have a dumb idea that having a baby would be wonderful, tell me to take a hike.' She glared at Scott. 'Or you have it.'

Scott kissed her forehead and wisely refrained from commenting.

Ally went for diversion. 'How long have you been married?'

'Two years,' Lisa ground out.

'We've been wanting a baby right from the beginning.' Scott grinned. 'Couldn't get it right.'

Ally chuckled. 'Babies are control freaks. They get conceived when it suits them, arrive when they choose, and they've hardly started. But you know what? They're wonderful.'

Under her hand Lisa's shoulders tensed as she yelled out in the pain of the next contraction.

'Lisa, breathe that gas in. You're doing brilliantly.'

The next hour passed slowly. Ally took observations regularly, noting them on Lisa's chart, occasionally going for a walk to the letterbox and back to give the couple a few moments alone, then returning to give Lisa more encouragement. Six o'clock clicked over on her watch. *There goes dinner with Flynn.* Even if Baby Ashton miraculously popped out right then, she'd be needed for a time. Guilt hovered in her head. Never before had she cared how long the birthing process took, she just loved being there with the mums, dads and their babies. But now she loved being with Flynn, too.

Her head jerked up. Loved being with him? Or loved Flynn, full stop?

'Ally, come quick. Lisa's pushing,' Scott called down the hall.

Good, focus on what's important. 'That's good, but we could be a while yet.' Though for Lisa's sake she hoped not. She was exhausted.

Examining her, Ally was happy to announce, 'Baby's crowning. When the urge to push comes, go with it. Don't try to hold back.'

'It's too damn painful to push,' Lisa yelled.

'Come on, Lisa. He's got to come out of there.' Scott reached for Lisa's hand and grimaced as she gripped him.

'Easy for you to say,' his wife snarled.

Ally had heard it all before. 'As soon as Ashton makes his appearance, you two will forget everything but your beautiful little boy.' This parenthood thing was awesome. Babies were amazing, so cute and vulnerable and yet bonding their parents in a way nothing else could.

Why hadn't her mother felt like that about her? Was her mother a freak? She was definitely the reason Ally would never have her own baby. What if the don't-love-your-own-baby gene was hereditary? There was no way on earth she'd chance having a child, only to dump her into the welfare system and disappear. And even if she did love her baby—which she was sure she would despite her past—she didn't know the first about raising one, about providing all the things a child needed, including loads of love. Her experience of babies stopped once she knew they were able to feed from mum's breast.

'Ally, I think he's coming,' Lisa broke into her thoughts, brought her back to the here and now, away from the daydreams of someone who should know better.

When Ashton slid into her hands, Ally felt tears prick her eyelids. 'Wow, look, Scott, he's lovely.' She lifted him to meet his parents. Her knees were shaky and her heartbeat erratic. 'He's the most beautiful baby I've seen.'

'Of course he is,' Scott whispered.

All babies were. She'd reacted the same way at that very first birth that had started her on the path to becoming a midwife. *Thank you, wee Lloyd, wherever you are now. Not so wee any more, I guess.* Mopping her eyes with her arm, she cleaned the mucus from Ashton and placed him on Lisa's breast.

Flynn picked her up a little after eight. She was tired and exultant. 'Another little baby safely delivered and in good hands.' She clicked her seat belt into place. 'Do you remember when you first held Adam?' That hadn't exactly changed the subject, had it? Darn.

'Everything about him—his scrunched-up face, his red skin, spiky black hair and ear-shattering cry. He hasn't changed much.' Flynn smiled with a far-away look in his eye.

'His face isn't red.' The love in Flynn's voice brought tears to her eyes and she had to look out the window at the houses they were passing until she got herself back under control. It was too easy to picture Flynn carefully cradling Adam wrapped in a blanket, like he was made of something so fragile he'd break at the slightest pressure. *I want that. No. I don't. I can't have it. It would be wrong for everyone.*

'Ally? Where've you gone?'

Suck it up, play the game. You know how to. 'I'm thinking pasta and garlic and tomatoes. It's been a long day and I forgot to buy my lunch on the way to work so missed out what with Baby Ashton stealing the show.'

'I'm sure Giuseppe will fix what's ailing you.' Flynn pulled up outside the restaurant.

'Good.' Pity there was no cure for what really troubled her. She could not, would not get too involved. Flynn had been hurt badly with Anna's death. So had Adam. She couldn't risk hurting them again. Forget involvement being a risk; hurting them would be a certainty. She was clueless in the happy-families stakes, and they so didn't deserve or need to be hurt by her. She shoved the door wide before Flynn had a chance to come round to open it for her. 'Let's go and have the night of our lives.'

'Ally.' Flynn's hand on her arm stayed her. 'You look absolutely beautiful tonight. More beautiful, I mean.'

'Thank you.' Her heart rolled. Talk about making everything harder. 'I went shopping yesterday.'

'I'm not talking about the dress, though you look stunning in it. It fits you like a second skin, accentuates all those curves I love touching.' He hesitated, breathed deep. 'But it's you that's beautiful—from the inside out.'

Nothing could've made her move at that moment if she'd tried. His words had stolen the breath out of her, liquefied her muscles, making them soft and useless. She was supposed to be having dinner with Flynn and then going back to his house and bed. He was not meant to be saying things that undermined her determination to stick to her rules—no deep, attaching involvement.

'Ally? Did I go too far?'

Yes, you did. Way too far. You're frightening me. Forcing a smile, she laid her hand over his. 'Thank you. That was a lovely compliment.'

'A heartfelt one. Now, let's enjoy ourselves and I'll stop the sentimental stuff since it seems to be upsetting you.' He hopped out of the car and strode around the front to her side.

She'd let him down. But what was a girl supposed to do? She couldn't take in what he'd said and start believing. That would be dangerous, but at the same time she couldn't walk away from Flynn tonight, or tomorrow, or any time during the next two weeks. No, she couldn't. Pushing out of the car, she laced her fingers through his and walked up the path to the welcoming door of the restaurant. 'I see the tide's farther in tonight. We won't be having our wicked way on the beach.'

Grinning, Flynn held the door wide and ushered her inside, whispering as she passed, 'You
give up too easily.'

Did she? 'I'm not going to ask what's on your
mind. I want to eat first.' She ran a hand over
his delectable butt before turning to follow the
same young waiter they'd had last week.

Giuseppe was there before they'd sat down.
'Welcome back, Ally. I'm glad you enjoyed our
food enough to return.'

'Come on, Giuseppe, how could I not?' She
kissed her fingertips. 'That carbonara was
superb.'

'The carbonara or the company you were keeping?' the older man asked with a twinkle in his
eye. 'By the way, you might be wanting this.'
He held up the half-full bottle of Merlot they'd
left on the beach.

Flynn laughed loudly. 'You old rascal. Who
found that?'

'I go for a walk along the beach every night
after I close the door for the last time.' Giuseppe
kept the bottle in his hand.

Uh-oh. What time had he closed the restaurant last Friday? Ally glanced across at Flynn,

saw the same question register in his eyes. Had Giuseppe seen them making out? She croaked out, 'Thank you. It seemed a waste not to have finished a good wine.'

Giuseppe nodded, his eyes still twinkling, leaving her still wondering what he'd seen, as he said, 'Tonight you will try something different. Something I recommend to match the meal I have arranged. This half-finished one you can take with you when you leave.'

Ally watched as he walked away, pausing at other tables to have a word with his guests. 'Do you think he knows?'

'That we made love on the beach? Yes, I suspect he does.' Flynn reached across and took her hand in both his. 'You know what? I couldn't care less.'

'Then neither do I.' And she wouldn't worry about anything else tonight either.

The meal was beyond superb and the wine excellent. The company even better. Flynn made her laugh with stories from his training days and she told him about going to school as an adult. It was a night she'd remember for a long time. It was intimate, almost as though they had a future, and she refused to let those bleak thoughts refuting that spoil anything.

'Here.' She twined her arm around Flynn's, their glasses in their hands. 'To a hot night under the stars. Tide in or out.'

Flynn smiled, a deep smile that turned her stomach to mush and her heart to squeezing. 'To a wonderful night under the bright stars with a special lady.'

But when they stepped outside there were no stars. A heavy drizzle had dampened everything and was getting heavier by the minute. 'You forgot to order the weather.' Ally nudged Flynn as they hurried to the car.

'Never said I was perfect.' He held the car door while she bundled inside.

No, but he wasn't far off. Leaning over, she opened his door to save him a moment in the rain. 'How long will it take you to drop off the babysitter?'

'Ten minutes.'

'That long?'

'You can warm the bed while I'm away.' Flynn laid a hand on her thigh. 'Believe me, I'll be going as fast as allowed.'

Heat raced up her thigh to swirl around the apex between her legs, melting her. 'Pull over.'

'What? Now? Here?' The car was already slowing.

'Right now and here.' She was tugging at his zip. Under her palm his reaction to her move was more than obvious.

'I haven't done it in a car since I was at high school.'

'Hope you can still move your bones, you old man.'

He growled as he nibbled the skin at her cleavage. 'Just wait and learn.' His hand covered her centre, his fingers did things that blanked out all the doubts and yearnings in her mind and made her cry with need, followed with release.

Flynn rolled onto his side, his arm under his head and his gaze fixed on the beautiful woman sleeping beside him. He was addicted to Ally Parker. There was no other word for what he felt. Addiction. He'd never known such craving before. The more he had of her, the more he wanted. His need was insatiable. If it wasn't so damned exciting it would be frightening. Frightening because it was filled with pitfalls.

He'd loved Anna beyond reason and had still failed her. If he hadn't been so damned determined to follow his career the way he'd wanted it she wouldn't have been in Melbourne that day and the accident wouldn't have happened. If he'd listened to her wishes, instead paying them lip service, his boy would still have his mother. That, more than anything, he could never forgive himself for. Every child deserved two parents, and especially their mother, to nurture them as they grew up.

And this had what to do with Ally? Ally already enjoyed being with Adam, didn't treat him as a pawn to get to his father but rather as an individual in his own right. She'd nurture and mother Adam if they got together.

A chill lifted goose bumps on his skin. He withdrew his arm and rolled onto his back to stare at the ceiling. They could not get together. Firstly, Ally didn't do settling down. That was so clear he'd be a fool not to acknowledge it.

He glanced across at her sleeping form. 'What happened that you can't stop in one place for more than a few weeks? Who hurt you so badly that you're prepared to miss out on what life's all about?' he whispered. 'Someone other than your mother?' That would be enough to knock anyone sideways for ever. But he had this niggling feeling he hadn't heard it all.

As the chill lifted and his skin warmed back to normal he ran a hand over her hair, rubbed a strand between his fingers. 'I would never hurt you, let you down.'

Huh? Hadn't he just reminded himself of how badly he'd let Anna down? Yep. And Adam. Adam. The crux of the matter. He'd do anything for his son. Anything. Which meant not getting too close to Ally, not seeking the answers to those questions in case they drove him on to making her happy, not sharing his life with her.

Ally rolled over, blinked open her eyes and smiled in a just woken up and still sleepy way. 'Hi,' she whispered.

'Hi, yourself.' He leaned in to place a light kiss on her brow, then her cheek, her chin, her lips. Two weeks. *Make the most of them. Stop analysing the situation and enjoy what's left.*

As he reached for her, the door flew open.

'Dad. Why was the door shut?' Adam shouted, loud enough for the whole island to hear as he pushed it wide.

'Good morning to you, too.' Flynn smiled and pulled the bedcovers up to Ally's chin. 'Hope you're okay with this,' he whispered to her. 'I forgot to relock the door after I went to the bathroom.'

'Not a problem, unless he wants to get in here with us,' she whispered back. 'Hello, Adam. How long have you been awake?'

'A long time. I've been watching cartoons.' Adam started to climb onto the bed.

Hell, Ally was buck naked. Adam was used to seeing him in the nude, but not a woman. 'Adam, can you pass Ally my robe? She's getting cold.'

'She should wear pyjamas to bed.'

How did Adam know she hadn't? Distraction needed. 'Let's have pancakes for breakfast.' That'd get his attention, pancakes being his all-time favourite breakfast food. *Unhealthy. Tough.*

'Ally, are you coming for a sleepover every night now?'

Flynn mentally threw his hands into the air. If

pancakes didn't work, then he had to get serious. 'Adam, go out to the lounge while we get up.'

Ally shook her head as though trying to make sense of everything. 'Sometimes when it's late I don't go home, but not every night. I've got my own place to go to.'

Adam nodded. 'I thought so. But if you want to stay every night we don't mind, do we, Dad?'

Which part of 'Go out to the lounge' hadn't he got? 'I guess not. Adam, we want to get up.'

'Okay. Are we having maple syrup and bacon on the pancakes?' Adam didn't look like he had any intention of moving this side of Christmas.

'We won't be having pancakes at all if you don't leave us.'

Under the covers Ally touched his thigh and squeezed it. 'Bacon, syrup *and* bananas. But I want to shower first and the longer we lie around, talking, the longer we're going to wait for our yummy breakfast.'

Adam nodded again. Where had this new habit come from? 'I'll get everything ready.'

'Great. See you out there soon.' Ally nodded back with a smile. 'But promise me you won't start cooking anything.'

'I don't know how to mix the flour and stuff.'

As Adam ran out of the room Flynn stared after him. 'He listens to you.'

'I'm a novelty. You're Dad.' Her hand stroked where a moment ago it had been squeezing.

'Keep that up and breakfast will be postponed for hours.'

She instantly removed her hand. Damn it. 'Hours? Talk about bragging.' She grinned at him. Then slid out of bed and wrapped herself in the too-large robe. 'I'm going to look so good sitting down to breakfast in my little black dress. Why didn't I think to bring a change of clothes?'

'You should leave a set here for the morning after.'

'If I did that, I wouldn't have many clothes left at the flat.'

She travelled light. Very light. 'Go shopping. Get some gear to keep here. In the meantime…' he swung his legs over the side of the bed, dug into his drawers for a sweatshirt and pair of trackpants '…try these for size.'

'I already know they'll be too long and loose around the waist, but my hips might hold them up.' She took the clothes and hugged them to her breasts. 'Who's first in the shower?'

'You go. I'll keep an eye on proceedings in the kitchen. Today could be the day Adam decides to try mixing the batter and that would be messy, not to mention uncookable.'

'You're not fair. He's got to have a go at these things. How else is he going to learn to look out for himself?'

'But it's so much quicker to do everything myself.'

Her face tightened and her chin lifted. 'In the long run you'll save heaps of time because Adam will be able to do these things for both of you.'

Ouch. She'd gone from Fun Ally to Serious Ally in an instant. She'd also had the nerve to tell him how his parenting sucked. 'Go and have that shower,' he ground out through clenched teeth.

He didn't want to start an argument by saying she should leave this to him, but it had nothing to do with her. Even if she might be right, Ally wasn't the one constantly working with a time deficit.

For a moment she stood there, staring at him.

Was she holding back a retort, too? Or formulating a whole load more criticisms? Or, heaven forbid, was she about to explain why she felt so strongly about his son learning to cook?

Not likely. She'd never do that. Ally was a closed book when it came to herself. Except for that one time of sharing her past hurts, what drove her, and what held her back, her past was still blurred. He needed to remember that—all the time. But right this minute he had to get back onside with her. They were spoiling what had been a wonderful night and should be a great day ahead. 'Ally, please, go and get cleaned up. Let's not waste the morning arguing.'

Her eyes widened. Then her stance softened, her shoulders relaxed. 'You're right. We've got pancakes and a morning at the wildlife centre to enjoy. And we'll need to stop at the flat on the way so I can put on some proper clothes.'

He'd dodged a slam dunk. 'Proper clothes? Since when weren't trackies and a sweatshirt proper?'

'Since fashion became important. In other words, since the first time a woman put on an

animal hide.' She grinned and his world returned
to normal.

His new normal. The one with Ally Parker in
it. The normal that would expire in two weeks'
time.

CHAPTER NINE

TUESDAY, AND ALLY parked outside the bakery just as her phone vibrated in her pocket. 'Hello?'

'It's Marie. I'm in labour.'

Her due date was in three weeks, but technically speaking Marie wasn't having her baby too early. Two weeks before due date was considered normal and nothing to be concerned about. 'I'm on my way. After I examine you we'll arrange to get you over to the mainland and hospital.'

'I doubt I'm going anywhere. The contractions are already coming fast.' Marie's voice rose with every word. 'Hurry, will you?'

'On my way. Try to relax. I know, easy for me to say, but concentrate on your breathing and time the contractions.' Great. The last thing Marie had said to her was that she never wanted to have a home birth. A friend of hers had had one last year and there'd been complications that had nearly cost the baby her life.

With a wistful glance at the bakery she jammed the gearshift in Reverse and backed out into the street.

Adam opened the door the moment she parked in Marie's driveway. 'Ally, Marie's got a tummyache. She's holding it tight.'

Adam was there. Of course he was. It was a weekday. He wasn't going to be anywhere else in the afternoon. 'Does Flynn know you've gone into labour?' she asked Marie the moment she stepped inside.

'No. I needed a midwife, not a doctor.' Marie glanced in the direction Ally was looking. 'Oh, Adam. He'll be fine. Anyway, what can Flynn do? Take Adam to the surgery for the rest of the day?'

'Surely Flynn's got someone he can ask to look after him?'

Marie's face contorted as a contraction gripped her. She held on to the back of a chair and screwed her eyes shut.

'Breathe deep. That's it. You're doing good.' Ally stepped close to rub her back and mutter inane comments until the contraction passed. Then she got down to business. 'Let's go to your bedroom so I can examine you. Adam, sweet-heart, Marie is having her baby so I want you to be very good for her. Okay?'

'She's having a baby? Really? Why does it hurt her?' His little eyes were wide.

'It's baby's way of letting everyone know it's coming.'

'Can I tell Dad?'

'Soon. I'm going with Marie to her bedroom.' His eyes filled with expectancy and she quickly stomped on those ideas. 'I want you to help me by getting things I need, like water or cushions or towels. But not until I ask you, all right?'

'Yes, I'll be good. Can I bring them into the bedroom?'

'No, leave them outside the door.' Hopefully Marie was wrong about her baby coming quickly and she'd soon be on her way to hospital. 'Why don't you watch TV until I call you?'

'I want to help.'

'I know, but first I have to check the baby, then I'll know what you can do for us.' If Marie was heading to hospital she'd drop Adam off at the medical centre. Flynn would sort out childminding. He must have made alternative arrangements for this eventuality.

Adam's mouth did a downturn, but he trotted off to the lounge and flicked on the TV.

'Thank you, Adam,' she called, before hurrying to Marie's bedroom and closing the door behind her. 'Have you called your husband?'

Tears welled up in Marie's eyes. 'My call went straight to voice mail. He's at sea on the fishing boat. This wasn't supposed to happen. He's booked leave for when the baby's due. He can't get here for days,' she wailed.

Ally gave her a hug and a smile. 'Well, in the meantime it's you and me. Unless you've got a close friend you'd like here, or family?' Someone familiar would make things work more smoothly.

'My family all live on the mainland and my girlfriend would be hopeless. Faints if there's the hint of blood or anyone's in pain.' Marie sank onto the bed as another contraction gripped her. 'I don't think I'm going anywhere. These contractions are coming too fast. I seriously doubt I've got time to get to the hospital.' Her voice was strained.

Ally glanced at her watch. She'd already begun timing the contractions. 'Four minutes. You're right, they're close.' She held Marie's hand until the current contraction passed. 'If you lie down I'll see what's going on.'

Marie flopped back onto the bed. 'I feel this pushing sensation, but I don't want a home birth. What if something goes wrong?'

'We have doctors only five minutes away. But you're jumping the gun. Baby might just pop out.' Ally mentally crossed her fingers as she snapped on vinyl gloves and helped Marie out of her panties. She wasn't surprised at the measurement she obtained. 'You're ten centimetres, fully dilated, so, yes, baby's on its way.' She calmly told her patient, 'Sorry, Marie, but hospital's definitely out. There isn't time.'

Marie's face paled and her teeth dug deep into her bottom lip. The eyes she lifted to Ally were dark with worry.

'Hey.' Ally wrapped an arm around her shoulders. 'You're going to be fine. I'll phone the surgery to tell them what's going on.' One of the doctors would be on notice to drop everything and rush here if anything went wrong.

'Sorry, I'm not good at this.' A flood of tears wet her cheeks.

'Find me a mother who is. This is all new to you. Believe me, no one pops their baby out and carries on as though nothing has happened. It's an emotional time, for one. And tiring, for another.' She sat beside Marie. 'Take it one contraction at a time. You've done really well so far. I mean it.'

Marie gripped Ally's hands and crushed her fingers as another contraction ripped through her.

'Breathe, one, two, three.' Finally getting her hands back and able to flex her fingers to bring the circulation back, Ally said, 'I'll get the gas for you to suck on. It'll help with the pain.'

'That sounds good. But I do need to push.'

'Try to hold off until I'm back. Promise I'll hurry.' She dashed out of the room and nearly ran Adam down in the hallway. 'Oops, sorry, sweetheart, I didn't see you there.'

'Is the baby here yet?'

'No.' But it wasn't too far away. 'Can you fill two beakers with water and leave them outside the door?' She had no idea if Marie wanted one, but giving Adam something to do was important.

His little shoulders pulled back as pride filtered through his eyes. 'I'll put them on a tray, like Dad does sometimes.'

'Good boy.' Out at the car she dug her phone out of her pocket and called the medical centre. 'Megan, it's Ally. Can you put me through to Flynn?'

'He's with a very distressed patient and said not to be interrupted unless it was an emergency.'

Define emergency. She guessed a baby arriving early didn't quite fit. 'When it's possible, will you let him know that I'm with Marie and she's having her baby at home? There isn't time to transfer her to hospital. Also mention it to Faye and Jerome in case I need help.'

'That's early. Tell her good luck from me. When Flynn's free I'll talk to him, but I suspect he's going to be a while. His patient is really on the edge.'

'Thanks, Megan, that'd be great.' She cut the receptionist off. Marie needed her. She gathered up the nitrous oxide tank, a bag of towels and another bag full of things she'd need.

'I'm still getting the water,' Adam called as she closed the front door.

'Good boy.' Back in the bedroom the temperature had dropped a degree or two. Sundown was hours away, but outside she'd noticed clouds gathering on the horizon. 'Marie, how are you doing?'

'Okay, I guess.'

'Here, suck on this whenever the pain gets bad.' Ally handed over the tube leading from the nitrous oxide tank. 'Have you got a heater we could use? I don't want baby arriving into a cold room, and I'd prefer to warm these towels as well.'

'There's an oil column one in the laundry. Adam knows where it is and can push it along on its wheels. It'll be perfect for what you're wanting.'

'Onto it.'

Outside the door Adam was placing the beakers ever so carefully on a tray he'd put on the floor earlier. 'Can you bring me the heater out of the laundry? Or do you want me to help?'

'I can do it. Do I have to leave it out here?'

'Yes, please.'

His little shoulders slumped. 'Why can't I see Marie?'

Ally knelt down and took his small hands in hers. 'When women have babies they don't like lots of people with them, watching what's happening. They get shy.'

'Why?'

'Because having a baby is private, and sometimes it hurts, and Marie wouldn't want you to see her upset.' *Sometimes it hurts?* Understatement of the century.

'No, she only likes me to see her laughing. I'll knock when I've got the heater.'

For a four-year-old, Adam was amazingly together about things. Nothing fazed him. But then he had lost his mother so he wasn't immune to distress, had probably learned a lot in his short life. He coped better than she did. He did have a great dad onside. 'Then you can play with all those toys I saw in a big box in the lounge.'

'But I like playing outside. Marie always lets me.'

'Today's different. I need you to play inside

today, Adam.' She held up a finger. 'Promise me you won't go outside at all.'

'Promise, Ally.'

Her heartstrings tugged. What a guy. As she gave him a hug a groan sounded from inside the bedroom. 'You're a champ, you know that?' *Now, please go away.*

'What's a champ?' Adam didn't seem to have heard Marie.

'The best person there is.' The groan was going on and on. 'I've got to see Marie.' *Please, go away so you don't hear this.* Nothing was wrong but that deep, growling groan might frighten him, or at least upset him.

Thankfully Adam had his father's sensitivity and recognised a hint when it came. He raced down the hall towards the laundry and Ally let herself back into the bedroom.

'Hey, how's it going?' The pain on Marie's scrunched-up face was all the answer she needed. 'Feel like pushing some more, I take it.'

'How can you be so cheerful?'

So they were at the yell-at-anyone stage. 'Because you're having a baby and soon you'll forget all this as you hold him for the first time. Can you lie back so I can examine you again?'

'Examine, examine—that's all you do.' But Marie did as asked.

Kneeling on the floor, she gently lifted Marie's robe. 'The crown's further exposed. Baby's definitely on its way.' She stood up and dropped the gloves into a waste bag. 'Have you tried to get hold of your husband again?'

'His name's Mark and, no, I haven't. He's not going to answer if he's on deck, hauling in nets. They don't have time.' Tears tracked down her face. 'Anyway, I want him here, not on the end of a phone.'

Ally picked up Marie's phone. 'How do we get hold of him? Can we talk to his captain?'

Marie stared at her like she'd gone completely nuts. Then she muttered, 'Why didn't I think of that?'

'Because you're having a baby, that's why.' Ally handed her the phone. 'Go on. Try every contact you've got.'

Just then another contraction struck and Marie began pushing like her life depended on it, all thoughts of phone calls gone.

'That's it. You're doing well.' Ally again knelt at the end of the bed, watching the crown of the baby as it slipped a little farther out into the world.

Knock-knock. 'I got the heater,' Adam called.

'Thank you. Now you can play with those toys.' She gave him a minute to walk away before opening the door and bringing the heater in. Plugging it in, she switched it on and laid two towels on top of the columns to warm for baby.

'Hello?' Marie yelled at someone on her phone. 'It's Marie, Mark's wife. I can't get hold of him and I'm having our baby. I need to talk to him.'

Ally held her hand up, whispered, 'Slow down, give the guy a chance to say something.'

Marie glared at her but stopped shouting long enough to hear a reply. 'Thank you so much. Can you hurry? Tell Mark to phone back on the landline so I can put him on speaker.' A moment later she tossed the phone aside, grabbed the edges of the bed and pushed again.

The phone rang almost immediately. Ally answered, 'Hey, is that Mark? This is Ally, Marie's midwife.'

'Hello, yes, this is Mark. What's up? Is she all right? The baby's not due for weeks.'

'Marie's fine. You can be proud of how she's handling this. Baby has decided today's as good as any to arrive.'

Marie snatched the phone out of her hand and yelled, 'Why aren't you here with me? I need you right now.' Then she had to drop it and clutch her belly.

Ally pressed the speaker button and Mark's voice filled the room. 'Hey, babe, you know I'd be there if I'd thought this would happen. How're you doing? Come on, babe, talk to me, tell me what's going on.'

'I'm having a baby, and it hurts like hell. It's nearly here and I can't talk any more. I've got to push.'

'Babe, I'm listening. Imagine me holding you against my chest like I did when you dislocated your shoulder. Feel my hands on your back, rubbing soft circles, whispering how much I love you in your cute little ear. Can you feel me there with you?'

Ally tried to block out this very personal conversation, pretend she was deaf, but those words of love touched her, taunted her. These two had a beautiful relationship. If Mark was a deep-sea fisherman, he was no softy, would definitely be a tough guy, and yet here he was speaking his heart to his wife when she needed him so much.

Marie cried out with pain, and pushed and pushed.

'Hey, babe, you're doing great. I know you are. You're a star. I'm not going anywhere until you have our little nipper in your arms, okay?'

Ally blinked back a tear and slipped out the door for a moment to get herself sorted. It wouldn't do for the midwife to have a meltdown in the middle of a birth. Not that that had ever happened but Marie's birth was affecting her deeply, more so than any other she'd attended. Leaning back against the wall, she took deep breaths to get her heart and head under control. *What was it like to have a man love you that much?* She could take a chance with a man like that. Even if she screwed up he'd be there to help her back onto her feet.

I want what Marie's got. Shivers ran through her and her skin lifted in goose-bumps. *No. I can't, don't, won't.*

Straightening up, she slapped away the tears and returned to her patient. Marie was still talking to Mark and didn't seem to notice her return. Had she seen her leave?

Then Marie was pushing again and this time there was no relief. Baby was coming and Ally prepared for it. 'The head's out. Here come the shoulders. That's it. Nice and gentle now.' She spoke louder so Mark could hear everything. Her hands were under the baby's head, ready for any sudden rush as the baby slid out into its new world. And then, 'Here he is, a beautiful boy. Oh, he's a sweetheart.'

Her heart stuttered. She'd called Adam a sweetheart earlier. It was one thing to say that about a baby she wouldn't be seeing much of, but Adam? He was wriggling into her heart without trying and soon she'd have to say goodbye.

'Can I hold him?' Marie asked impatiently, reaching out.

'In a moment. The APGAR score's normal.' Ally gently wiped away vernix, mucus and blood spots from his sweet little face.

'Give him to me, give him to me. Mark, we've got a boy. He's gorgeous. Looks like his dad.'

Ally rolled her eyes as she placed the baby on Marie's swollen breasts. 'I need him back in a moment to weigh him.'

Mark was yelling out to his crewmates, 'It's a boy. I'm a dad.' And then he was crying. 'Wish I was with you, babe. Tell me everything, every last detail. Are we still going to name him Jacob?'

'Well, I can't name him after our midwife so I guess so. I think it suits him.' Marie was laughing and crying and drinking in the sight of her son lying over her breast.

'Here comes the placenta.' Ally clamped it and cut the cord. 'I need to examine you once more, then I'll cover you up and let you talk to Mark alone for a bit.' Adam would be getting lonely out in the lounge. She'd make him a bite to eat, poor kid.

Her examination showed a small tear. 'You need a couple of stitches. Nothing major,' she added when worry entered Marie's eyes. 'It often happens in fast deliveries.'

'Right.' Marie went back to talking to Mark, the worry gone already.

Ally quietly went about retaking Jacob's

APGAR score. His appearance and complex-
ion were good. Counting his pulse, she tried not
to listen in to the conversation going on between
Jacob's parents, concentrating on the sweet bundle of new life. Her heart swelled even as a snag
of envy caught her again. She could have it all
if only she found the right man. Flynn instantly
popped up in her head. Losing count, she started
taking Jacob's pulse again, this time totally concentrating and pushing a certain someone out
of her skull.

'Pulse one hundred and ten. Good.' She flicked
lightly on Jacob's fingers, watched as he immediately curled them tight. 'Reflex good, as is
his activity.' His little legs were moving slowly
against his mother's skin, and she couldn't resist
running a finger down one leg. He hadn't done
more than give a low gasp but his chest was rising and falling softly. So his respiratory effort
was okay. Ally wrote down her obs and then
dealt with the tear while Marie carried on talking.

She found Adam in the lounge, despondently
pushing a wooden bulldozer around the floor.

He leapt up the instant he saw her with the rubbish bag. 'Ally, has the baby come?'

'Yes, and it's a little boy.'

Adam stared up at her. 'Can I see him now?'

'I can't see why not.' She took his hand and walked down to Marie's room, saying to the new mum, 'You've got your first visitor.' And then her heart squeezed.

Marie was cuddling her precious bundle and trying to put him on the breast. 'I hope Jacob takes to this easily.'

'Don't rush. It takes time to get the hang of it.' She went to help position Jacob.

Marie smiled down at her boy. Then looked up. 'Hello, Adam, want to see Jacob? Come round the bed so you can see his face. Isn't he beautiful?'

'Can I hold him?' Adam hopped from foot to foot and Ally saw the hesitancy in Marie's expression.

'Not today. He's all soft and needs careful holding. But tomorrow you can. He'll be stronger then.'

Adam stood close to Marie and stared at the baby. Slowly he placed one hand very carefully on his tiny arm and stroked it. His mouth widened into a smile. 'Hello, baby.'

Ally's eyes watered up. She'd never forget this moment. Adam's amazement, Marie's love, Jacob so tiny and cute. She'd seen it before, often, but today it was definitely different. Not because she'd begun to see herself in Marie's place, holding her own precious bundle of joy. Definitely not because of that.

She stood there, unable to take her gaze away from the scene, unable to move across to the towels that needed to be put into a bag for the laundry company. Just absorbing everything, as though it was her first delivery. The incredible sense of having been a part of a miracle swamped her. *Could I do this? Give birth myself?* Having a baby wasn't the issue. She'd be fine with that. But everything after the moment she held that baby in her arms—that was the problem. Did she have mothering instincts? Or had she inherited her mother's total lack of interest when it came to her own child, her own flesh and blood?

She couldn't afford to find out. It wouldn't be fair on her baby if she got it wrong.

'Marie, you certainly don't waste time when you decide you're ready to have your baby.' Flynn strode into the room and came to an abrupt halt. 'Adam, what are you doing in here?'

CHAPTER TEN

'DAD!' ADAM JUMPED up and down. 'Marie's got a new baby. I think it hurt her.'

'What?' Flynn spun around, his face horrified, and demanded, 'How does he know that?'

Ally stepped up to him. 'Adam did not see the birth, if that's what you're thinking.'

'Then explain his comment.'

Ally backed away from the anger glittering at her. 'He asked why he couldn't come in here and I said that having a baby is private and sometimes it hurts a little.' She had not done anything wrong.

Marie was staring at Flynn like she'd never met him before. 'For goodness' sake. Do you think either of us would've allowed him in here while I was giving birth? Seriously?'

Flynn shoved a hand through his hair, mussing it up, except this time that didn't turn Ally on one little bit. 'I guess not.'

'Dad, I helped Ally. I got water and the heater.'
Flynn's mouth tightened.

Ally told him, 'Adam left everything outside the door. The closed door.' Why can't he see the pride shining in his son's eyes? She ran a hand over Adam's head. 'My little helper.'

Flynn flinched. 'Sorry for jumping to conclusions, everyone.' He was starting to look a little guilty. 'I never did do anything about making alternative arrangements for this eventuality.' He gave Marie a rueful smile. 'Now can I meet Jacob?'

Reluctantly Marie handed the baby over. 'Only for a minute. I don't like letting him out of my arms.'

Ally watched Flynn's face soften as he peered into the soft blue blanket with its precious bundle, and felt her heart lurch so hard it hurt. There was so much love and wonder in his expression she knew he was seeing Adam the day he'd been born. It was a timely reminder that she didn't have a place in his life.

Spinning around, she shoved the baby's notes at Marie. 'I'll make that coffee I promised.' Like when?

Marie was quick, grabbing her hand to stop her tearing out of the room. Her eyes were full of understanding. 'White with two sugars.' She nodded and let Ally go.

Thank you for not outing me.

Flynn was oblivious anyway, so engrossed in Jacob that it was as though no one else was in the room.

When she returned with three coffees he was reading the notes and only grunted, 'Thanks,' at her. Guess he'd finally worked out where his loyalties truly lay, and they weren't with her.

Ally asked Marie, 'Is there anything you want me to do? Washing? Get some groceries in?'

Flynn answered before Marie could open her mouth. 'No need. Marie's mother will be here soon.'

Marie gaped at him. 'Tell me you didn't phone her.'

Colour crept into Flynn's cheeks and another dash of guilt lowered his eyebrows and darkened his eyes. He was having a bad afternoon. 'With Mark at sea for another week, you need someone here. Who better than your mother?'

'You know the answer to that,' Marie growled. 'Ring her back and tell her to turn around.'

'You don't think this is an opportune time to kiss and make up?' Flynn asked. 'Estelle sounded very excited about the new baby.'

Ally looked from Marie to Flynn. What was going on here? They knew each other well, but for Flynn to be telling Marie to sort her apparent problem with her mother could be stretching things too far. Time for a break from him. Taking Adam's hand, she said, 'Come on, let's get you some food. I bet your tummy's hungry.'

'It's always hungry.'

She glanced at Flynn as she reached the door and tripped. He was staring at her with disappointment in his eyes. 'What?' she demanded in a high-pitched voice.

He shook his head. 'Nothing.'

Hadn't she been telling herself what she and Flynn had going was only a short-term fling? If she needed proof, here it was.

In the kitchen Ally put together enough sandwiches for everyone. She got out plates and placed the food on them. Next she put the kettle on to make hot drinks all round. All the while she was trying to ignore that look she'd seen in Flynn's eyes.

Adam chomped through two sandwiches in record time.

'Slow down or you'll get a tummyache.'

'No, I won't. My tummy's strong.' He banged his glass on the table.

Ally smiled tiredly at the ring of milk around his mouth and ignored the tug at her heart. 'Wipe your face, you grub.'

Flynn strode into the kitchen and picked up one of the sandwiches, munched thoughtfully.

'Dad, can I see the baby again?'

'Of course you can. But be very careful if you touch him. He's only little.' Flynn watched his son run down the hall, a distant gleam in his eyes making Ally wonder what he was thinking. When Adam disappeared into Marie's room he closed the kitchen door and she found out. 'Marie's very happy with how you handled the birth. Said you were calm and reassuring all the time.'

'I'm a midwife, that's what we do. It's in the job description.'

'What I don't condone is my son's presence in

the house at the time. He shouldn't have been with Marie from the moment she went into labour. Why couldn't you have gone next door to see if Mrs James could look after him?'

'One, there wasn't a lot of time. Two, as I don't know Mrs James, I'm hardly going to leave a small boy with her. Your small boy at that. You could've arranged for someone to come and collect him. You did get my message?' Two could play this game.

'Why didn't you get Megan to arrange someone?'

'It's not my place to make demands of your receptionist.'

Flynn didn't flinch. 'What was Adam doing while you were occupied with Marie? You weren't keeping a proper eye on him, were you?'

'You know what? Adam isn't my responsibility.' She was repeating herself, but somehow she had to get through that thick skull. Except she suspected she was wasting her time. Maybe shouting at him might make him listen. But as she opened her mouth her annoyance faded. She didn't want to fight with him.

'But you were here. You could've taken a few

moments to find a solution. Marie's baby wasn't going to arrive that quickly.'

Maybe he had a point, and she had made a mistake. 'I'm sorry. I got here as soon as I could after Marie phoned to say she'd gone into labour. Everything was hectic and Adam was happy watching TV.' But she should've thought more about Adam. Just went to show how unmotherly her instincts were. 'I did my best in the situation. I explained to Adam what was happening and he was happy to bring towels and water to leave outside the bedroom door. Not once did he see anything he shouldn't.'

'He's a little boy.' Flynn wasn't accepting her explanation. 'He'd have heard her cries and groans. It's not a massive house.'

'He was safe. I didn't put him in a position where he'd be scared, and I honestly don't think he was.' Her guilt increased. She should've thought more about Adam's age, should've tried harder to find a solution. He might've heard things a young child was better off not hearing. What if he had nightmares about it? But he'd been excited to see Jacob, not frightened of the baby or Marie. But there was no denying she'd got it wrong. Apparently she should've seen to Adam before Marie.

Ally shivered. Forget thinking she might have her own baby. She wasn't mother material. Having never had the parental guidance that would've made her see how she should've cared for Adam had shown through this afternoon. One thing was for sure, she wouldn't be any better with her own.

At least she could be thankful that she'd had a reminder of that now and not after she'd given in to the yearning for her own baby that had begun growing inside her. She would not have her own children. That was final. She squashed that hope back where it belonged—in the dark, deep recesses of her mind, hopefully to stay there until she was too old to conceive.

Flynn waited until Marie's mother arrived before he took Adam home. *Talk about being a spare wheel.* Ally and Marie talked and laughed a lot, getting on so well it reminded him of Anna with Marie. Ally had fussed over the baby while his mum had taken a shower, but handed Jacob back the moment Marie returned to her bedroom. She hadn't been able to entirely hide the longing in her eyes.

Flynn had tried to deny the distress he'd seen in Ally's face earlier. The distress that had changed to bewilderment and lastly guilt—brought on by him. The guilt had still been there whenever she'd looked at him, which was probably why she'd kept her head turned away as much as possible. He'd become the outsider in that house. Marie and Jacob and Adam had got all her attention. And he'd hated that. So he'd taken Adam and left. *Like a spoilt child.*

Now at home he swore—silently so Adam didn't pick up any words he'd then be told off for using. Then he deliberately focused on his son and not the woman who had his gut in a knot and his head spinning. He really tried. *Adam, my boy. I love you so much I'm being overprotective. But that's better than not caring.*

If ever there was a woman he could've expected to look out for Adam it was Ally. Not to mention Marie. He'd seen that stunned look on Marie's face when he'd given Ally a hard time. Of course Marie would know how unusual it was for him to lose his cool.

He cracked an egg and broke the yolk. 'Guess that means scrambled eggs and not poached.' He found a glass jug and put the pan away. Broke in some more eggs, whisked them into a froth and added a dash of milk. 'Adam, want to put the toast on?'

'Okay, Dad.' His boy stood on tiptoe at the pantry, reaching for the bread. 'Why isn't Ally sleeping over?'

Because your father's been a fool. 'She's tired after helping Jacob be born.'

'I like Jacob.'

Adam sounded perfectly happy, as if being around while a birth was going on was normal. And why wouldn't it be? Ally had made sure Adam wasn't affected by seeing anything untoward.

Flynn put the eggs into the microwave. *Ally, I'm so sorry for my rant. It was my responsibility to look out for my son, not yours, or anyone else's.* Ever since Anna's death he'd been determined to be the best dad he could to make up for Adam not having a mother. Hell, that's why they lived on the island and he did the job he did.

Yet today he'd been quick to lay the blame right at Ally's feet for something that bothered him.

Sheba rubbed her nose against his thigh and he reached down to scratch behind her ears. 'Hey, girl, I've made a mess of things.' Picking up his phone, he punched in Ally's number. His call went straight to voice mail. 'Ally, it's Flynn. I'd like to talk to you tonight if you have a moment.'

But he knew that unless she was more forgiving than he deserved, she wouldn't call. Action was required.

'Adam, want to go and see Ally?'

The shout of 'Yes!' had him turning the microwave off and picking up his keys. 'Let's go.'

Despite the absence of the car in Kat's drive, Flynn still knocked on the front door and called out. 'Ally? Open up.'

Adam hopped out and added his entreaties but Ally wasn't answering.

Flynn doubted she'd be hiding behind the curtains. That wasn't her style. Ally wasn't at home.

Back on the road Flynn headed to town to cruise past the restaurants and cafés. 'There.' He pointed to a car parked outside the Chinese takeaway and diner.

'Yippee, we found her.' Adam was out of the car before Flynn had the handbrake on.

'Wait, Adam.' Though Ally was less likely to turn away from his son, he had to do this right or there'd be no more nights with her in his bed, or meals at Giuseppe's, or walks on the beach. *There aren't going to be many more anyway. She leaves at the end of next week.* He wouldn't think about that.

She sat in a corner, looking glum as she nodded her head to whatever music was playing through her earphones.

'Ally, we came to see you.'

Her head shot up when Adam tapped her hand. 'Hey.' She smiled directly at his son. 'Are you here for dinner?' Did she have to look as though she really hoped they weren't?

Flynn answered, 'Only if it's all right with you.'

Her eyes met his. No smile for him as she shrugged. 'I only need one table.'

'We'd like to share this one with you.' He held his breath.

Adam wasn't into finesse. He pulled out a chair and sat down. 'What can I have to eat, Dad?'

Flynn didn't take his gaze off Ally, saw her mouth soften as she glanced at his son. He said, 'I apologise for earlier. I was completely out of line.'

She didn't come close to smiling. 'Really?' Her gaze returned to him.

He took a chance and pulled out another chair. 'Really. I should've had something in place for today—for whatever day Marie had her baby. Adam is my responsibility, no one else's. It's been on my list to arrange another sitter but I never got around to it.' Much to his chagrin. He twisted the salt shaker back and forth between his fingers. 'I was angry for stuffing up, and I took it out on you. I apologise for everything I said.'

Ally pushed the menu across the table, a glimmer of a smile on her lips. 'I only ordered five minutes ago.'

That meant she accepted his apology, right? 'Adam, do you want fried rice with chicken?'

'Yes. Ally, are you coming for another sleepover tonight?'

Flynn's stomach tightened. *Too soon, my boy.*

Too soon. We need to have dinner and talk a bit before asking that.

Ally shook her head. 'Not tonight. I need to do some washing and stuff.' She was looking at Adam, but Flynn knew she was talking to him.

Two steps forward, one back.

She hadn't finished. 'Besides, I'm always extra-tired after a delivery and need to spend time thinking about it all.' Her voice became melancholy, like she was unhappy about a bigger issue and not just about what he'd dumped on her earlier.

He gave the order to the woman hovering at his elbow and turned to lock eyes with Ally. 'What's up?' How could he have been so stupid as to rant at her? Now she wasn't staying the night, and who knew when she'd be back at his house, in his bed? Actually, he'd love nothing more than to sit down with a coffee or wine and try some plain old talking, getting to know each other better stuff. When she didn't answer he continued, 'What does a birth make you think about?'

'Everything and nothing. That whole wonderful process and a beautiful baby at the end of it. Like I told you the other day, I find it breathtakingly magical.' Her finger was picking at a spot on the tabletop. 'Yet I'm the observer, always wondering what's ahead for this new little person.'

'Do you want to have children someday?' Didn't most people?

The finger stopped. Ally lifted her head and looked around the diner, finally bringing her gaze back to him. 'No.'

'You'd be a great mother.'

Silence fell between them, broken only when Ally's meal arrived. But she didn't get stuck in, instead played with the rice, stirring and pushing it around the plate with her fork.

Adam asked, 'Where's my dinner?'

Flynn dragged his eyes away from Ally and answered. 'We ordered after Ally so it will be a few more minutes.'

Ally slid her plate across to Adam. 'Here, you have this one. It's the same as what you ordered.'

'You sound very certain—about no children of your own,' Flynn ventured.

'I am.'

'That's sad.'

'Believe me, it's not. If I'd had a child, that

would be sad. Bad. Horrible.' The words fell off her trembling lips.

He couldn't help himself. He took her hand in his and was astonished to feel her skin so cold. 'Tell me.'

'I already did.' She'd found a point beyond his shoulder to focus on.

While he wished they were at home in the comfort and privacy of his lounge, he kept rubbing her hand with his thumb, urging her silently to enlighten him, let out what seemed to be chewing her up from the inside. 'Only that you were abandoned. Doesn't that make you determined to show yourself how good you'd be?'

Their meals arrived and they both ignored them.

'My mother didn't want me. I grew up in the welfare system. Moved from house to house, family to family, until I was old enough to go it alone.' Her flat monotone told him more than the words, though they were horrifying enough.

'Your father?'

'Probably never learned of my existence—if my mother even knew who he was.'

'You know,' Flynn said gently, 'your mother

may have done what she did because she *did* love you. If she wasn't in a safe situation, or wasn't able to cope, it might have been that giving you up was her way of protecting you. Haven't you ever worked with women in that position?'

'Yes,' Ally admitted slowly. 'But if it was love, it didn't feel much like it to me.'

Flynn hated to think of Ally as a kid, adrift in the foster-care system without a steady and loving upbringing. It wasn't like that in all cases, he reminded himself. Anna's brother and sister-in-law had two foster-children that they loved as much as their own three. But look at Ally. Adorable, gorgeous, kind and caring. What's not to love about her? Was that his problem? Had he fallen for her? Nah, couldn't have. They'd only known each other a little more than two weeks. Hardly time to fall in love, especially when they knew nothing about each other. Except now he did know more about Ally than he would ever have guessed. And he wanted more. He could help her, bring her true potential to the fore.

Ally tugged her hand free, picked up her fork. 'See? You're speechless. It's shocking, but that's who I am, where I come from, what I'll always

be. Now you know. You were right. I shouldn't
have been in charge of Adam, even if by proxy.
I know nothing about parenting.'

No. No way. Flynn grabbed both her hands,
fork and all. 'Don't say that. I'd leave Adam with
you any day or night. Today was me being precious. Since Marie and I are friends, I felt a little
left out. Plain stupid, really.'

Ally tried to pull free, but he tightened his
grip.

Finally she locked the saddest eyes he'd ever
seen on him. 'Are we a messed-up pair, or what?'
she whispered.

*I'm not messed up. I get stuff wrong, but I think
I've done well in moving on from Anna's death
and raising our son.*

'I am determined to do my absolute best for
Adam, in everything.'

'You're doing that in spades.'

'So why do I feel guilty all the time?'

Her brow furrowed. 'About what?'

About Adam not having his mother in his life.
'I try to raise him as his mother wanted.' This
was getting too deep. He aimed for a lighter
tone. 'Eating raw vegetables every day and never

having a sweet treat is too hard even for me, and I'm supposed to make Adam stick to that.' *But it isn't always what I want, or how I'd bring my boy up.*

Her fingers curled around his hands. 'That's not realistic. Even if you succeed at home, the world is full of people eating lollies and ice cream, roast vegetables and cheese sauces.' At last her eyes lightened and her mouth finally curved into a delicious smile that melted the cold inside him.

The smile he looked for every day at work, at night in his house. 'Like Danish pastries, you mean.'

'You've got it.' Her shoulders lifted as she straightened her back. Digging her fork into her rice, she hesitated. 'I haven't known you very long, but it's obvious how committed you are to your son, and how much you love him. Believe me, those are the most important things you can give him.'

Said someone who knew what it was like to grow up without either of those important things. He answered around a blockage in his throat,

'Thank you. Being a solo dad isn't always a level road. Scary at times.'

'It's probably like that when there are two parents. Come on, let's eat. I'm suddenly very hungry.'

'Something you and Adam have in common. You're always hungry.' The last hour being the exception.

She grinned around a mouthful of chicken and rice.

His stomach knotted. He loved that grin. It was warm and funny. But now he understood she used it to hide a lot of hurt. Hard to imagine her childhood when he'd grown up in what he'd always thought of as a normal family. Mum, Dad and his brothers. No one deliberately hurt anyone or was ungrateful for anything. Everyone backed each other in any endeavours. When Anna had died he'd been swamped with his family and their loving support to the point he'd finally had to ask them to get back to their own lives and let him try to work out his new one.

'Dad, can I have ice cream for pudding?'

Ally smirked around her mouthful.

'Gloating doesn't suit you.' He laughed. 'Yes,

Adam, you can. Ask that lady behind the counter for some while Ally and I finish our dinner.'

As Adam sped across the diner, probably afraid he'd be called back and told to forget that idea, Flynn watched him with a hitch in his chest and a sense that maybe he was getting this parenting stuff right after all.

'Good answer,' said Ally.

'Would you change your mind about a sleepover?' Might as well go for broke. After being so angry with Ally, then getting the guilts, all he wanted now was some cuddle time. Yeah, okay, and maybe something hotter later. But seriously? He wanted to be with Ally, sex or no sex.

Her smile stayed in place. 'I meant it when I said I get exhausted after a delivery. And I do like to think it all through, go over everything again.'

Huge disappointment clenched his gut but he wouldn't pressure her. 'Fair enough. But if you decide you need a shoulder to put your head on during the night, you know where to find me.' Huh? What happened to no pressure? 'If you want company without the perks, I mean.' He smiled to show he meant exactly what he'd said, and got a big one in return.

'You have no idea how much that means to me. But this is how I deal with my work. I'm not used to dumping my thoughts on anyone else.'

'You should try it. You might find it cathartic.' Next he'd be begging. 'Tell me to shut up if you like.'

She took his hands in hers, and this time her skin was warm. Comfort warm, friendly warm. 'I'm not used to being with a man every night of the week. I'm used to my own company and like my own space. Don't take it personally, it's just the way I am.'

Sounded awfully lonely to him. 'I'll cook you dinner tomorrow night.' When would he learn to zip his mouth shut? 'If you'd like that.'

'It's a date. I'll bring dessert. Something Adam will love.'

'You're corrupting my kid now?'

'You'd better believe it.'

CHAPTER ELEVEN

'YOU LOOK WORSE than the chewed-up mess my cat dragged in this morning,' Megan greeted Ally the next morning when she walked into the surgery. 'Not a lot of sleep going on in your bed?'

'No. I tossed and turned for hours.'

'Haven't heard it called tossing and turning before, though I see the resemblance.' Megan laughed.

'Trust me, I was very much alone. Is everyone here yet?' Was Flynn here? He mightn't have kept her awake in the flesh, but she'd spent hours thinking about him. Hours and hours. Nothing like her usual night after a birth.

'I think they're all in the tearoom.'

Ally looked at the list of her appointments for the morning. 'At least there's no chance of falling asleep at my desk with all these women to visit.'

In the tearoom a large coffee from her favourite coffee shop was set at what had become her place. 'Thanks,' she muttered, as Flynn nodded to her. He was the only one in there.

'I was out early visiting Marie and Jacob so Adam and I had breakfast at the café.'

Ally chuckled. 'Now who's spoiling him?' Then wished the words back as his smile dipped. 'Spoiling's good. Who's looking after Adam today?'

'A friend on the other side of the island. She's had him before when Marie needed to go somewhere little boys weren't welcome.' Flynn pulled her chair out.

Sinking onto it, she lifted the lid on her coffee and tentatively sipped the steaming liquid. 'That's so good. Caffeine's just what I need. If I hadn't been running late I'd have stopped for one myself.' So Flynn had lots of friends he could call on. Lucky man. But friends also meant staying in touch, being there when needed, opening up about things best left shut off. *Has he changed how he feels about me now that he knows the truth?* 'Is Adam happy to go to this lady?'

'Absolutely. He gets to take Sheba so they can go for walks in the park with Gina's two spaniels.'

Cosy. Did the woman have a husband? *Down, green monster, down. You have no right poking your head up.* So far her night-time lectures to herself about falling in love with a man who was out of reach didn't seem to have sunk in. Slow learner. *Flynn is totally committed to Adam and his job. There is no room for you in his life.* She repeated what she'd said over and over throughout the night. And again it didn't make a blind bit of difference. Try, *There's no room for Flynn and Adam in your life. They live in the same place every day of the year. You move somewhere new so often you're like a spinning top.*

'Morning, Ally.' Faye strolled into the room. 'I hear Marie's baby arrived in a bit of a hurry.'

'He sure did. And he's absolutely gorgeous.' She couldn't wait to visit this morning.

'Humph. Babies are all the same to me. Cry and poo in their nappies a lot. Very uninteresting at that age.'

Ally blinked. Had she heard right? 'You haven't

had your own children?' All babies were beautiful, even if some were more so than others.

'Got three of the blighters. Love each and every one, but that doesn't mean I thought they were cute when they arrived.'

What a strange lady. But at least she was there for her kids and probably did a lot with them. 'How was Marie this morning?' She looked at Flynn.

'Arguing with her mother about who was bathing Jacob.' He grinned like he'd been naughty. Which he had. If not for him Marie's mother wouldn't be there. 'But at least they're talking, which is a vast improvement.'

Jerome joined them and the meeting got under way. Thankfully it was short as Ally was itching to get on the road and go visiting patients, to get away from that distracting smile of Flynn's. As she headed to the door and her car, he called, 'You still on for tonight?'

'I'm buying the dessert after my house calls.' She shouldn't join him for the whole night, but she couldn't resist. This had been a fling like no other she'd ever had. This time she dreaded finishing it and heading away. Not that she wanted to stay put on Phillip Island for however long the fling took to run its course either. But there was this feeling of so much more to be done, to share with Flynn, to enjoy with his son.

For the first time in her adult life she didn't want to move on. For the first time ever a person had got under her skin, warmed her heart in a way it had never been warmed. It made her long for the impossible—a family she could truly call her own.

She should've said no, that she'd be staying home to wash her hair.

But there was no denying the liquid heat pouring through her body just at the thought of a night with Flynn. So—how could she leave next week without shattering her heart?

It's too late. Might as well grab every moment going. It'd be silly to go through the rest of my time here staying in the flat, being miserable. Miserable would come—later, back on the mainland.

'Chocolate Bavarian pie.' Ally placed the box she'd bought in the supermarket on Flynn's bench. 'It's defrosted and ready to go.' She bent down to scratch Sheba's ears. 'Hey, girl, how're you doing? Recovered from that run yet?'

Lick, lick. Yes or no? Sheba had struggled a bit as they'd loped along the beach early yesterday morning.

Flynn slid a glass of red wine in her direction. 'Merlot tonight. Goes with the sausages I'm cooking.' He grinned that cheeky grin that got to her every time. 'They're beef.'

'Beef and red wine. A perfect combination,' she said with her tongue firmly in her cheek. That navy striped shirt he wore with the top button open to show a delectable V of chest was also perfect. Just enough visible chest to tantalise and heat her up in places that only Flynn seemed able to scorch. She winked. 'What time does Adam go to bed on Fridays?'

'Half past nine,' Flynn told her, straight-faced.

She spluttered into her glass. 'Half past nine? You've got to be kidding me.' Three hours before she could get her hands on the skin under that shirt? She'd combust with heat.

'Yep, I am.' Then he grinned again. 'You're so easy to wind up.'

'Phew. For a moment there I thought I'd have

to lock him in the lounge with Sheba and race you down the hall for a quickie.'

Desire matching hers flicked into his eyes. 'Now, there's a thought.'

This banter she could do. It was easy and fun and how flings were run. 'Guess I'd better stick to wine for now.'

'We're invited to Jerome's tomorrow night for an indoor barbecue, along with the rest of the staff. But he specifically asked us as a couple.'

The air leaked out of her lungs. This might be something she couldn't do. It hinted at something more than a casual relationship, like a date involving his colleagues and friends. Colleagues and friends who'd read more into the situation than was there. Was Jerome playing matchmaker? 'That's nice.' Well, it would be under other circumstances.

'You're not happy?'

She shrugged. 'I'm sure it will be fun, but maybe I'll give it a miss.'

A furrow appeared between his eyes. 'I accepted for both of us.'

'Then you'll have to *un*accept.' What had happened to consulting her first?

'Why? You've been working with everyone for three weeks so what's the big deal?' Then that furrow softened. 'I get it. The *couple* word. That's what's got your knickers in a twist, isn't it?'

'So what if it has? We're not a couple. Not in the true sense. We're having an affair. Next weekend it will be over. How do you face your colleagues then, if they're thinking we've got something more serious going on?'

How do I look Megan in the eye next week and say of course we're only friends. Even friends with benefits doesn't cover it. I'm falling for you and I need to be pulling back, not stepping into a deeper mire.

'Ally, relax. Everyone's aware you're moving on and I'm staying put. Jerome thought it would be more comfortable for you to go with me as there will be others there you haven't met. That's all there is to it.'

'You're ignoring that *couple* word.' Didn't it bother him? Because he was so comfortable in his life that he thought it ludicrous to even consider he was in a relationship?

Flynn set his glass carefully on the bench and

ran his fingertip over her lips. 'Sure I am. It was the wrong word to use. We've spent a lot of time together since you turned up on the beach that first day. You've given me something special, and I'm going to miss you, but we've both known right from that first kiss that whatever we have between us would never be long-term. I don't care what anyone else thinks. It's no one's business.'

Where was the relief when she needed it? Flynn had saved her a lot of hassle by saying what they had going was a short-term thing. But the reality hurt. A lot. In her tummy, especially in her heart. Her head said the best thing for everyone was that she'd be leaving. Her heart said she should stay and see if she could make a go of a relationship with Flynn and his son.

'Ally? Would you please come to the barbecue with me as my partner for the night?' When she didn't answer he added, 'People know we've been seeing each other—going out for meals, taking Adam to the beach and other places. It's not as though this is going to be a shock for them or the source of any gossip.' He drew a breath and continued. 'I want this last week with you.' His smile was soft and yet determined. It arrowed right into her chest, stabbed her heart.

And made everything even more complicated.

How could she say no when she wanted it, too? In the end it was Flynn who'd be left to face any gossip. In the end it would be agony to leave him whether she went out with him again or not. She had to grab whatever she could and stack up the memories for later. 'I'd love to go with you,' she said quietly.

The days were flying by and Ally was withdrawing from him. Flynn hated it. Sure, she still came home with him for the night, but there seemed to be a barrier growing up between her and them as a twosome. She'd already begun moving on in her mind. There, he'd said it. He'd started denying the fact she would be leaving soon, even when it was there in black and white on the noticeboard in this office. Kat would return home on Friday—tomorrow. She'd take over the reins on Saturday and Ally would leave the island and head for her next job. He knew all that. He'd signed the contract with Ally's employers.

But knowing and facing up to what her leaving truly meant were entirely different. He refused to admit the other half of his bed would be cold and empty again. Wouldn't contemplate sitting down to an evening meal with only Adam for company. Daren't think how he'd fill in the weekends without her laughter and eagerness for fun pulling him along.

'That needs photocopying so the hospital in Melbourne have records.' Ally dropped a file beside Megan. 'Hey, Flynn, got a minute?'

'Of course.' *Always got hours for you.* Had he been hasty in thinking she was putting space between them? Did she have a plan for what they might do on her last nights?

'I'm concerned about Chrissie.'

So much for plans and hot farewells. 'Come into my office.' He nodded at the patients sitting in the waiting room.

Ally got the message. 'Sure.' The moment she stepped inside his room she spun to face him. 'Chrissie's doing great physically. But she's got attached to me already and that's not good. She says she doesn't want to see Kat.'

'Strange. Kat gets on with everyone.' Like Ally. 'Did she give a reason?'

'Something about Kat's sister and Chrissie being rivals at school.' Ally shrugged those shoulders he'd spent a long time kissing last night. 'I was wondering if you could see her, maybe talk sense into her. I've explained that Kat would never tell her sister a single thing about the pregnancy, but Chrissie's not wearing it.'

'I'll talk to Chrissie, maybe with Angela there.' But he wondered how much of this had to do with Kat and how much was due to the way Chrissie had taken to Ally. 'You handled the situation very tactfully and sympathetically at a time when Chrissie was beside herself with worry. This could be about her not wanting you to leave.' He didn't want her going. Adam wouldn't, either.

A soft sigh crossed Ally's lips. 'There's not much I can do about that. I am going.'

'I know.' All too well. 'Do you ever get tired of moving on?'

Her eyes met his and she seemed to draw a breath before answering. 'No. It's how I live and there's a certain simplicity to not owning a house or a truckload of furniture or even a carful of clothes.' She looked away.

Flynn couldn't read her. He wanted to know if she felt sad about leaving him, or happy about another job done and their affair coming to an end. But as he started to ask his heart knocked so hard against his ribs he gasped. *I love her. I love Ally Parker. I'm not wondering any more. I know.* Asking her about her feelings just became impossible. She might ask some questions in return, questions he still wasn't ready to answer.

So he continued to study her while not being able to lock gazes with her, and he thought he saw no regret in her stance, her face or her big eyes. So Ally hadn't come to love him in the way he had her. Pain filled him, blurred his vision for a moment. Rocked him to the core. How could he have fallen in love with Ally? He'd never believed he'd love again, and yet it only taken a few short weeks. Had it happened that first day when Sheba had dumped her on the beach?

Ally's soft voice cut through his mind like a well-honed blade. 'I'd better get a move on. I'm going to weigh Jacob this morning.'

He watched her retreating back, his hands curled into fists to stop from reaching after her. So much for thinking she might reciprocate his feelings. It wasn't going to be at all difficult for her to walk away.

Ally stayed in the shower until she heard Flynn and Adam leave for their walk on the beach with Sheba. She'd cried off, saying she had a head-ache. That was no lie. Behind her eyes her skull pounded like a bongo drum. Her hands trembled as she towelled herself dry. Her knees knocked as she tried to haul her jeans up her legs. It was Saturday.

'Goodbye, Flynn.' She hiccupped around the solid lump of pain in her throat. 'Bye-bye, Adam. Be a good boy for your dad.' *I will not cry. I don't cry. Ever.*

Reaching out blindly, she snatched a handful of tissues and blew her nose hard, scrubbed at her eyes. One glance at her hands and she knew it'd be a waste of time trying to apply make-up. 'Go plain Jane today.' What did it matter any-way? It wasn't as though she'd be seeing Flynn.

Tears threatened and she took as deep a breath

as possible. 'Suck it up, be tough, get through the day. Tomorrow will look a whole heap better.'

Now she'd taken to lying to herself. But if it got her out of the house and on the road before Flynn and Adam returned, then it was the right thing to do.

Yesterday she'd packed up her few possessions and the bags sat in the boot of the medical centre's car. The key to Kat's flat was back under the flowerpot on the top step, her contact details written on a pad inside in case she'd left anything behind. Now all she had to do was drive to the surgery to dump the car and be on her way.

But she turned the car in the direction of Marie's house. 'One last cuddle with Jacob.' So much for leaving unobtrusively. But she couldn't bring herself to turn away yet.

Marie opened her front door before Ally had time to knock. 'Hey, you're out and about early.'

'Yeah, thought I'd see everything's okay with you.'

'Come in. Want a coffee?' Marie headed for the kitchen. 'Jacob's just gone down.'

'Then I probably should carry on.'

There was already a mug of steaming coffee

on the bench and Marie poured another without waiting to see if Ally wanted it. 'We had a good night. Jacob only woke four times.' She grinned.

'How do you manage to look so good after that?' Ally paced back and forth.

'Mark's coming home today.' Marie slid the mug in Ally's direction. 'Excuse me for being blunt but *you* look terrible. What's up?'

'Nothing.' She tried to shrug, but her shoulders were too heavy.

'Ally, I don't know you well, but something's not right. Has Flynn done something wrong?'

'No. Not at all.' She'd gone and fallen in love with him, but that didn't make him a bad man. She was the fool.

'Good, I'd have been surprised. He thinks the world of you and would do anything for you. Apart from that hiccup the day Jacob was born.'

Coming here had been a mistake. 'I'd better go. I've to be somewhere. Thanks for the coffee.' Which she hadn't even tried. 'I'll see myself out.'

'Don't go,' Marie called.

Ally shut the door behind herself and ran to the car.

A taxi dropped her off at the ferry terminal

half an hour later. Once on board she found an empty seat out of the way of the happy hordes and pushed her earbuds in, turned up the music on her music player and pretended all was right with her world. Except it wasn't, as proved by the onset of deep sobs that began racking her body as the ferry pulled out. Her fingers dug into the palms of her hands and she squeezed her eyes tight against the cascade of tears.

Someone tapped her knee. 'Here. Have these.' An older woman sitting opposite handed her a pack of tissues.

'Th-thanks,' she managed, before the next wave of despair overtook her.

Flynn. I love you so much it's painful.

Flynn. What I wouldn't give to feel your arms around me one more time.

Flynn. I had to go. It wouldn't have worked.

For every wipe at her face more tears came, drenching the front of her jersey. 'I love you, Flynn Reynolds,' she whispered. Shudders racked her body from her shoulders all the way down to her feet.

This was terrible. The last time she'd cried

when moving on had been the day she'd left her favourite foster-family—the Bartletts.

The woman opposite stirred. 'We're docking.'

Ally blew her nose and swiped her eyes once more, drew a breath and looked up. 'Thank you again.'

'You'll be all right?'

'Yes, of course.' Never again. With one last sniff she inched forward in the queue to disembark and headed for her real life; the one she'd worked hard to make happen and that now seemed lonely and cold.

Flynn felt a chill settle over him the moment he turned into his street. Ally's car was gone. Somehow he wasn't surprised but, damn it, he was hurt. How hard would it have been to say goodbye?

Spinning the steering wheel, he did an about-turn and headed for Kat's flat to say to Ally the goodbye she hadn't been willing to give him.

But it was Marie's car outside Kat's flat, not the one Ally had been using. As soon as Flynn pulled up Marie was at his window. 'Do you know where Ally's gone?'

'I hoped she'd be here.' He was too late.

'She came to my place about an hour ago. She was very upset. I tried to find out why, but she left again. In a hurry, at that. That's why I came around here.'

Flynn's mouth soured. Ally was upset? Why? *Did you want to stay on? With me? No, that was going too far.* 'I'd say she's on the ferry, heading home.' Except she didn't have a home to head to. Just a bed she borrowed on a daily basis.

'Flynn, what's going on? Why's Ally upset? As in looking like she was about to burst into tears?' Marie's voice rose.

Ally and tears didn't mix. He'd never seen her close to crying. *Duh.* There hadn't been any reason for it. His gut clenched. If Ally was crying, then he wanted to be with her, holding her, calming her down and helping sort whatever her problem was. 'She's finished her contract with us, but from what I've learned about her that wouldn't be the reason for her being unhappy.'

Marie clamped her hands on her hips. 'Unhappy? Broken-hearted more like. Downright miserable.' She stared at him. 'A little bit like how you're looking, only more so.'

'I look miserable? Broken-hearted?' Here he'd been thinking he could hide his feelings. But, then, most people didn't know him as well as Marie did.

Marie's stance softened. 'You love her, don't you?'

Ouch. This might not go well, Anna having been Marie's best friend and all. 'You don't pull any punches, do you?'

'Have you told Ally?'

He shook his head.

'What's held you back? Anna? Because if that's the case, you have to let her go. The last thing Anna would've wanted would be for you to be on your own for the rest of your life.'

Flynn growled, 'Since when did you become my therapist?'

She smiled. 'Just being a good friend. So? Spill. Why haven't you talked to Ally about this?'

'All of the above. And Adam. I'm totally focused on giving him everything he needs in life and I don't know if there's room for Ally. But, yes, I love her, so I guess I'll be making space.' Over the past weeks he'd begun to feel comfortable living here, enjoying his work more. Without Ally, life wouldn't be as much fun.

'I hope you come up with a more romantic approach when you tell Ally all this.' Marie leaned in and brushed a kiss over his chin. 'Adam adores Ally, and vice versa. What's more, he needs a mother figure in his life. You're not so hot on the soft, womanly touch.'

'Thank goodness for that.' Flynn felt something give way deep inside and a flood of love and tenderness swamped him. *Ally, love, where are you?* 'She's afraid she isn't mother material.' When astonishment appeared on Marie's face, he hurried to add, 'She's a welfare kid, lived in the system all her childhood.'

'Oh, my God. Now I get it. She was running from you. She doesn't want to make things any worse for you.'

'Yep, and I let her go.' Actually, no, he hadn't. He'd fully expected Ally to be waiting when he and Adam had got back. He should've known better. If he hadn't diverted to the vet's to pick up dog shampoo, would he have been in time to see her before she'd left? 'Marie, thanks, you're a treasure. Now, go home to that baby of yours and tell your mother to leave before Mark gets here.'

'On my way. What are you going to do?'

'Adam and I are taking a trip.'

CHAPTER TWELVE

'THE COFFEE'S ON,' Darcie said as she buzzed Ally into the apartment building.

'Hope it's stronger than tar,' Ally muttered, as she waited for the lift that would take her to the penthouse. She was wiped out. All those tears and that emotional stuff had left her exhausted. No wonder she tried so hard not to get upset.

The apartment door stood wide open as Ally tripped along the carpet to her latest abode, and she felt a temporary safety from the outside world descend.

'Hey, how's things?' Darcie appeared around the corner, took one look at her face and said, 'Not good. Forget coffee. I think this calls for wine.'

A true friend. 'Isn't it a bit early? It's not quite eleven yet.'

'It's got to be afternoon somewhere in the world.'

Good answer. 'I'll dump my bags.' And dip my face under a cold tap. But when Ally looked into the bathroom's gilt-edged mirror she was horrified at the blotchy face staring back at her. 'Who are you?' she whispered.

Cold water made her feel a little more alive but no less sad. She found her make-up and applied a thick layer in a misguided attempt to hide some of the red stains on her cheeks. Quickly brushing her hair and tying it up in a ponytail, she went out to Darcie. 'Sorry about that. I needed to freshen up a bit.'

Darcie immediately handed her a glass of Sauvignon Blanc. 'Let's go out on the deck. The sun's a treat for this time of year.'

She followed, blanking out everything to do with Phillip Island and Flynn, instead trying to focus on what might've been going on at the midwifery centre while she'd been away. 'Tell me all the gossip. Who's gone out with who, who's leaving, or starting.'

Sitting in a cane chair, Darcie sipped her wine and chuckled. 'You won't believe what's happening.'

Ally sprawled out on the cane two-seater,

soaked up the sun coming through the plate-glass windows, and tried to relax. Darcie was very understanding. She'd wait to be told what was going on in Ally's life. And if Ally never told her she wouldn't get the hump. A rare quality, that. Exactly what Ally needed right now. 'Great wine.' She raised her glass towards Darcie. 'Cheers.'

At some point Darcie got up and made toasted sandwiches and they carried on talking about the mundane.

It was the perfect antidote to the tumultuous emotions that had been gripping Ally all morning. There was nothing left in her tanks. She'd given it all on Phillip Island, left her heart with Flynn and his boy. Thank goodness she had tomorrow to recover some energy and enthusiasm for work before turning up at the midwifery unit on Monday.

Then Darcie spoilt it all. 'Who's this Flynn you keep mentioning?'

Ally sat up straight. 'I don't.'

Darcie held her hand up, fingers splayed. 'Five times, but I'm not counting.'

I can't have. I would have noticed. 'He's one of the doctors I've been working with.'

'Yet I don't recall you mentioning any of the others. Guess this Flynn made an impact on you.'

You could say that. 'Okay, I'll fess up and admit to having a couple of meals with him and his wee boy.'

Darcie said nothing for so long Ally thought she'd got away with it and started to go back to her relaxed state.

Until, 'Ally, what else do you do when you're not being a midwife?'

That had her spine cracking as she straightened too fast. 'Isn't that enough? I'm dedicated to my career.' Apart from shopping for high-end clothes and getting in the minimum of groceries once in a while, what else was there to do?

'Your career shouldn't be everything. Don't you ever want a partner? A family? Your own home? Most of us do.'

'I'm not most of you.'

'What about this Flynn? Do you want to see him again?'

Yes. But she wasn't about to admit that. 'No,' she muttered, hating herself as she lied.

'You haven't fallen in love with him, have you?'

And if I have? Ally raised her eyes to Darcie and when she went to deny that suggestion she couldn't find the words. Not a single one.

'I see. That bad, huh?' Darcie leaned back in her seat. 'I don't know what's gone on in your life, Ally, and I'm not asking.' She paused, stared around her beautiful apartment before returning her gaze to Ally. 'Sometimes we have to take chances.'

Ally shook her head. 'Not on love,' she managed to croak.

'Loving someone can hurt as much as denying that love. But there's always a chance of having something wonderful if you accept it.'

There really wasn't anything she could say to that so she kept quiet.

The buzzer sounded throughout the apartment, its screech jarring. Darcie stood up. 'That's probably Mary from the ward. We're heading out to St Kilda for a few hours. Want to join us?'

Ally shook her head. 'Thanks, but, no, thanks.

I've got a couple of chores to do and then I'm going to blob out right here. But with coffee, not wine.'

She tipped her head back and closed her eyes, pulled off the band from her ponytail and shook her hair free. Her hand kneaded the knots in her neck. What was Flynn doing? Had he taken Adam around to see Jacob? Her heart squeezed. *I miss you guys already.*

'Hello, Ally.'

She jerked upright. 'Flynn?' Couldn't be. Her imagination had to be working overtime.

'Ally, we came to see you.' No mistaking that excited shriek. Or the arms that reached for her and held tight.

Not her imagination, then. Adam was here. *Flynn* was here. Meaning what? Lifting her head, she stared at the man who'd stolen her heart when it was supposed to be locked away. The man she'd walked away from only hours ago without a word of goodbye or a glance over her shoulder—because any of those actions would've nailed her to the floor of his home and she'd still be on Phillip Island.

Adam tightened his hold. 'I'm missing you,

Ally. You didn't wait for us.' Out of the mouths of babes—came the truth.

Her head dropped so her chin rested on Adam's head. 'Adam, sweetheart.' Then her throat dried and she couldn't say a word. Finally, after a long moment of trying not to think what this was about, she raised her eyes to find Flynn gazing at her like a thirsty man would a glass of cold water on a hot day. The same emotions she'd been dealing with all day were glittering out from her favourite blue eyes. 'Flynn,' she managed.

'Hey.' He took a step closer. 'The house didn't feel the same when we got back from our walk. Kind of empty.' Flynn didn't sound angry with her, but he should. She had done a runner.

She owed him. 'I'm really sorry but I couldn't wait.' *If I did I'd never have left*. Her heart seemed to have increased its rate to such a level it hurt. 'It's an old habit. Get out quick. Don't look back.'

Bleakness filled his gaze, his tongue did a lap of his lips. 'I see.'

Adam wriggled free of her arms and sat on the floor beside her.

Flynn didn't move, just kept watching her.

Suddenly Ally became very aware that this was the defining moment in her life. Everything she'd faced, battled, conquered, yearned for— it all came down to now and how she handled the situation. She loved Flynn. Before— *Gulp*. Before she told him—if she found the courage—she had to explain. 'It's an ingrained habit because of all those shifts I made as a child. I learned not to stare out the back window of the car as my social worker took me away from my latest family to place me in the midst of more strangers.'

Flynn crossed to sit in the chair Darcie had been using earlier. He still didn't say a word, just let her take her time.

Her chest rose and fell as she spoke. 'I know it's not the same as what I did today, that you do care about me and never promised me anything that you haven't already delivered, but I come pre-conditioned. I'm sorry.'

'You were waiting for one of those families to adopt you.' Flynn looked so sad it nearly brought on her tears.

Adam, who shouldn't be taking the slightest

notice of this conversation, stared up at her and asked, 'What's adopt mean?'

'Oh, sweetheart. It's when people give someone else a place in their family, share everything they've got, including, and most importantly of all, their hearts.'

'Don't you have a family?' He'd understood far too much.

'No, Adam, I don't.'

'We can adopt you. Can't we, Dad?'

Ally's mouth dropped open. Her stomach tightened in on itself. Her hands clenched on her thighs. What? No. Not possible. He didn't understand. It wasn't that simple.

She leapt up and charged across to the floor-to-ceiling window showcasing Melbourne city. Her heart was thudding hard, and the tears that should've run out hours ago started again.

'Ally.' A familiar hand gripped her shoulder.

She gasped. 'You've taken your ring off.' Could she start believing?

He tugged gently until she gave in and turned around. But she couldn't look up, couldn't face the denial of Adam's silly statement if it was staring at her out of Flynn's eyes. 'Ally, look at me. Please.'

Slowly she raised her head, her eyes downcast, noting the expanse of chest she'd come to know over the last month, the Adam's apple that moved as Flynn swallowed, that gorgeous mouth that had woken every part of her body and could kiss like no other man she'd known. Expelling all the air in her lungs, she finally met Flynn's gaze. There was no apology there, no *It's been nice knowing you but we don't want to know you any more*. All she found was love. Genuine love, deep love that spelled a bond and a future if she dared take it.

'Flynn,' she whispered. 'I have to tell you something.' The breath lodged painfully in her chest, but if she was going to gamble, then she had to start by being honest. 'Today was different. For the first time ever I didn't want to go. That's why I ran.' Tremors rippled through her. This was way too hard. But there was a lot to lose—or gain. A deep breath and she continued. 'I've fallen in love with you. Both of you.' And then she couldn't utter another word as tears clogged her throat.

His arms came around her, held her loosely so he could still watch her face. 'This is the last time you're walking away. You're not on your own any more. You have me, us. We are your family.' His mouth grazed hers.

'You want to adopt me?' she croaked against his lips, being flippant because she was afraid to acknowledge what he'd said for fear his words would vaporise in a flash.

'Try amalgamate. We want to bring you in with us, make us a threesome, a family.'

'Amalgamate? Sounds like a business deal.' But the warmth lacing his voice was beginning to nudge the chill out of her bones. 'I'll bring two bags of clothes and my music player and you'll supply a home.' She smiled to show she wasn't having a poke at him. Then she gasped and dashed to her bag to pull out the dogs. 'Plus these two. I take them everywhere. This time when I put them on the shelf they'll stay there so long they'll gather dust.'

Flynn looked ready to cry. 'That's the closest you've got to owning a pet?' His arms came around her again.

'Bonkers, eh?'

He stepped back, shoved his hand through his hair. 'You have no idea how much I mean every word. I love you so much it hurts sometimes.'

She gasped. Had Flynn said he loved her?

He hadn't finished. 'I could've told you that days ago, but I got cold feet. I put Adam before everything else. Which I have to do, but I used him as an excuse not to let you know where my feelings for you were headed. I didn't want you to leave, yet I didn't know how to tell you that. I think I was kind of hoping you'd just hang around and that would solve my dilemma.'

She stared at him as a smile began breaking out across her lips, banishing the sadness that had dominated all day. 'You said you love me.'

'Yes, Ally, I did. I mean it. I love you.'

'No one's ever told me that before.' Oh, my goodness. Flynn loved her. But it wouldn't feel so warm and thrilling and wonderful if she didn't love him back. '*I've* never loved anyone before.' There hadn't been anyone to bestow that gift on. 'This love is for real, I promise.'

'Hey, I can see it in your eyes. It's been there for days if only I'd known what to look for.'

'Adam, look away. I'm going to kiss your father.'

'Why?'

'Because I love him.'

'Do you love me?'

'Absolutely.' She bent down to press a kiss on his forehead. 'Yes.' When she straightened Flynn was waiting for her, his arms outstretched to bring her close. His head lowered and his mouth claimed hers.

This kiss was like no other they'd shared. This was full of promises and love and life.

'How long are you going to kiss Dad?' Adam tapped her waist.

'For ever,' she murmured against Flynn's mouth, before reluctantly pulling away. She was afraid to let him go. She needed to keep reassuring herself he'd always be there.

Flynn took her hand and laced their fingers together. 'Want to come home with us for the rest of the weekend?'

'I can't think of anything I'd rather do.'

'Thank goodness.' Until he'd relaxed she hadn't realised how tense he'd become.

'I have to be back here on Monday.'

He nodded. 'But now you have a home to go to when you're not on a job.'

Her heart turned over. 'You're not expecting me to give up working for the midwifery unit, then?'

'You'll do that when you're good and ready. We've got all the time in the world to learn to live together and for you to feel right at home on the island. I won't be rushing you, sweetheart.' Then he really stole her heart with, 'When I say I love you, I mean through the best times and the worst, through summer, winter and Christmas and birthdays. I'm here for you, with you, Ally, for ever.'

'But what if I fail? This will be new for me.'

'You won't fail, Ally. You'll make mistakes.'

'Fine. What happens when I make these mistakes?' she asked, her heart in her mouth.

'We sort them and we move on. Together.'

Her heart cracked completely open. Could she do this? 'Can I do this? Really?' She locked her eyes on the man who'd turned her world on its head.

'Your call, sweetheart. But I believe you can do anything you set your mind to.'

Was Flynn not as scared as she was? For all his understanding, maybe he didn't get it. But looking into those eyes she'd come to trust, she saw nothing but his confidence in her. He trusted her to look out for Adam to the best of her ability, even if that ability needed fine-tuning along the way. He trusted her to love him as much as she'd declared. Her mouth was dry. Finally she managed to croak, 'Let's go home.'

'Yes.' Adam jumped up and down, then ran circles around the lounge. 'Yes, Ally's coming back home with us.'

Flynn reached for her, his smile wobbly with relief. 'Home. Our home. The three of us.' Then his smile strengthened. 'And the dogs.'

Eighteen months later...

Ally laid baby Charlotte over her shoulder and rubbed her tiny back. 'Bring up the wind, sweetheart, and you'll feel so much better.'

Flynn grinned. 'Look at you. Anyone would think you'd been burping babies for ever. Charlotte is completely relaxed lying there.'

Ally's heart swelled with pride and happiness. 'Seems I got the mothering gene after all.'

Flynn's grin became a warm, loving smile. 'Ally, I was never in doubt about that. I've seen you with Jacob, with Chrissie's Xavier and half the other new babies on the island. You're a natural when it comes to making babies happy.'

She blinked back a threatening tear at his belief in her. That belief had helped her through the doubts that had reared up throughout her pregnancy, had meant he hadn't hovered as she'd learned to feed and bath and love her baby. And Adam. Well. 'Adam's been complaining this morning. Apparently I should've made a boy so he had a brother to play football with.'

'He'll have to wait a year or two.'

'We're having more?'

'Why not?'

She blinked. That told her how much he believed in her. In her chest her heart swelled even larger.

The bed tipped as Flynn sat down beside her and reached for his daughter. 'Hello, gorgeous.' He laid Charlotte over his shoulder and held her with one hand.

'Hello,' said Ally, her tongue in her cheek.

He leaned over and kissed her. 'Hello, gorgeous number one. Did you get any sleep last night?'

'An hour maybe.' Charlotte had had colic and nothing had settled her. But Ally had been happy, pacing up and down the house, cuddling her precious bundle, kissing and caressing. Just plain loving her baby. She'd known what to do, hadn't had any moments of doubt when Charlotte wouldn't settle. And this morning she was being rewarded with a contented baby.

Yep, she did have the right instincts. When Charlotte had been born three weeks ago she'd been stunned at the instant love and connection she'd felt for her baby. It had been blinding in its strength. For the first time ever, Ally realised how hard it must have been for her mother to give her up. She might have desperately wanted to keep her baby but had been too scared, troubled or unable to support herself. Now, as a mother, Ally knew it wasn't a decision any woman would make lightly. She'd never know the reason her mother had left her on that doorstep. But now at last, with Flynn by her side, she was moving on, making a loving life for her family and herself.

'Flynn.' She wrapped her hands around his free one. 'I love you so much. I'm so lucky.'

'You and me both, sweetheart.'

'Let's get married.' She hadn't thought about it. The words had just popped out, but she certainly didn't want to retract them.

His eyes widened and that delicious mouth tipped up into a big smile. 'That's the best idea you've had since we decided to get pregnant.'

'I thought so.' Her lips kissed the palm of his hand, and then his fingers. Life couldn't get any better.

* * * * *

MILLS & BOON®
Large Print Medical

January

Unlocking Her Surgeon's Heart	Fiona Lowe
Her Playboy's Secret	Tina Beckett
The Doctor She Left Behind	Scarlet Wilson
Taming Her Navy Doc	Amy Ruttan
A Promise...to a Proposal?	Kate Hardy
Her Family for Keeps	Molly Evans

February

Hot Doc from Her Past	Tina Beckett
Surgeons, Rivals...Lovers	Amalie Berlin
Best Friend to Perfect Bride	Jennifer Taylor
Resisting Her Rebel Doc	Joanna Neil
A Baby to Bind Them	Susanne Hampton
Doctor...to Duchess?	Annie O'Neil

March

Falling at the Surgeon's Feet	Lucy Ryder
One Night in New York	Amy Ruttan
Daredevil, Doctor...Husband?	Alison Roberts
The Doctor She'd Never Forget	Annie Claydon
Reunited...in Paris!	Sue MacKay
French Fling to Forever	Karin Baine

MILLS & BOON®
Large Print Medical

April

The Baby of Their Dreams	Carol Marinelli
Falling for Her Reluctant Sheikh	Amalie Berlin
Hot-Shot Doc, Secret Dad	Lynne Marshall
Father for Her Newborn Baby	Lynne Marshall
His Little Christmas Miracle	Emily Forbes
Safe in the Surgeon's Arms	Molly Evans

May

A Touch of Christmas Magic	Scarlet Wilson
Her Christmas Baby Bump	Robin Gianna
Winter Wedding in Vegas	Janice Lynn
One Night Before Christmas	Susan Carlisle
A December to Remember	Sue MacKay
A Father This Christmas?	Louisa Heaton

June

Playboy Doc's Mistletoe Kiss	Tina Beckett
Her Doctor's Christmas Proposal	Louisa George
From Christmas to Forever?	Marion Lennox
A Mummy to Make Christmas	Susanne Hampton
Miracle Under the Mistletoe	Jennifer Taylor
His Christmas Bride-to-Be	Abigail Gordon